A HUNDRED THOUSAND WORDS

BY

NYRAE DAWN

Published by

Nyrae Dawn

This book is a work of fiction. Names, characters, places and incidents are products of the author's imagination or are used fictitiously. Any similarity to actual persons, living or dead is coincidental and not intended by the author.

Printed in the United States of America.

All products/brand names mentioned are registered trademarks of their respective holders/companies.

Cover Image by: mimagephotos #54357303/Deposit Photos

Edited by: Edie Danford

Formatted by: Angel's Indie Formatting

DEDICATION

This book is dedicated to anyone who has ever felt different for any reason. To anyone who has ever crushed on someone from afar.

And to anyone who has ever feared losing those they love.

You only live once. Make it count.

CHAPTER ONE

It was my best friend's older brother who made me realize I'm gay. Sure, I'd wondered before. I mean, a part of me had to have known, but it was Levi who made me admit it to myself. Or rather, it was the fact that when I really started jerking off on the regular, it was to thoughts of him. It didn't matter that he was an asshole—a straight-as-straight-could-be asshole—he was the star player in a whole hell of a lot of my fantasies growing up.

But then I went away for college and made all of those fantasies and more come true. Not with Levi because of the whole being a straight asshole thing, but once I was out of Coburn, the small town in Oregon where I grew up, I didn't need to pine after the guy I'd never have. I was in San Francisco for fuck's sake. Home had a shortage of gay guys to choose from, but San Francisco was an all-you-could-eat buffet.

Now it's winter break and I'm home from college, so of course the Levi-factor is in effect again. His family is throwing a holiday party and I'm sitting on their living room couch watching Levi do what he does best: charming a group of women. He must be telling some kind of joke or something because they're laughing and smiling, all eyes pinned on him. He was always the golden child—straight A's in school, popular, good at sports. Maybe that's why I wanted him so much. He was everything I wasn't. Not that I want to be those things, because I don't, but on him they're sexy as hell.

He flashes a smile at his admirers that gives me a tingle in my balls. Groaning, I try to look away but can't. He's always had this magnetic energy that sucks me in.

His hickory-brown hair has grown out since I saw him last. It's hanging in his face, almost blocking his dark eyes. When he grins, big and bright, his thin lips stretched wide, the group does the same, smiling at him. It's like when someone yawns and you're powerless not to yawn yourself. Sometimes it's as though he lends you some of his confidence, or at least I tell myself that. I'm pretty sure I'm not the only one who feels that way as everyone looks at him like he's teaching them to hang the moon. But then he has to go overboard when he puts his arms out, flexing his biceps. That's when I roll my eyes and look away.

"What a fucking idiot." My best friend Chris sits next to me on the couch. We met in fifth grade and we've been tight ever since. I was the quiet kid before I met Chris. Take after my dad that way, I guess, but Chris pulled me out of my shell.

We were always doing something stupid when we were kids. Nothing too outrageous: got caught drinking and smoking a few times, missing curfew. He stole two Playboy magazines for us to jack off to, which was when I first realized there was something different between the two of us. Naked girls and tits did nothing for me. I pretended to come as hard as he told me he did, and then a few months later, I was forgoing the magazines in favor of mental images of his brother.

"Eh," I reply, because talking about Levi with Chris never goes well. He's always had issues with his brother.

"Watch them, though—women eat him up. I don't fucking get it. I swear to God if Gemma falls for him I'm going to beat his ass."

Laughing, I look at Chris. His hair's the same shade of brown as Levi's but it's shorter. Chris has always had this jealousy thing with his brother, which I guess is probably normal. I don't have siblings so I wouldn't know. His concerns aren't too farfetched, though. Every girl who spends more than five minutes with Levi ends up falling for him. I can see why Chris would be jealous, especially because Chris had been in love with some of them. Or at least, he'd wanted to screw them. There was one girl in particular who Chris had been into. They'd fucked around a few times and the next thing we knew, Levi was taking her out. Chris hasn't forgiven him for that one.

"I'm sure your girl isn't going to fall for your brother." If I don't change the subject, he'll go off on all the ways he can't stand Levi, and I'll want to stab my eardrums so I don't have to hear it all for the millionth time. Nudging him, I say, "It's kind of good to be home for winter break. I missed this."

This being his family. My dad was around and he tried his best, but it wasn't easy for him to support us. He worked all the time to make ends meet, and Chris's family let me pretend like I belonged there because Chris and I were close. It made things easier on Dad. He misses Mom more every time he looks at me.

"When will Gemma be here?" I ask. Chris went and fell in love our sophomore year of college. Since I'm in San Francisco and Chris's school is back East, this break will be the first time I meet her.

Before he replies, loud laughter erupts from the other side of the room and I glance over to see Levi sitting by the table with his head tilted back, letting out belly laughs. I watch his throat move. He has a really sexy throat I wouldn't be averse to kissing...and I really need to shut my goddamned brain down and stop lusting after Chris's brother. Even if there was a chance in hell I could bang Levi, I'm pretty sure Chris would lose his fucking mind if I did. Chris is the best friend I've ever had, my only real one, and I wouldn't sacrifice that for anything.

"A few days. She's incredible, Toby. You'll love her. I can't wait for you to meet her." Chris nudges me the same way I nudged him a minute before, so I pull my attention away from Levi and back to him. "What about you? You said there were all kinds of dudes to choose from at school."

While I'm glad he feels comfortable talking to me about this, discussing my sex life with him isn't something I'm in the mood to do. With Chris it's all roses and hearts and love. With me it's ass and hands and mouths. Big difference in what we're looking for.

"There were plenty of guys." I wink. "So many, in fact, I feel like I'd be doing them a disservice if I got serious about any of them. Who buys the first car they test drive?" That's what going off to school was about for me. Yes, there's the education, but I really wanted to *live* and experience all the shit I couldn't while at home. I'm the only queer guy in my small town—the only one I know of, anyway—and I never

7

had an opportunity to experience much of anything before leaving for San Fran.

Portland, which isn't far away, has a great gay population, but it wasn't always easy for me to get there when I was younger.

Chris has always been sympathetic to my situation in Coburn, but my brand of loneliness isn't something he can really understand. It's easier not to mention it much.

Still, he's really the only person I have in my life who wants to be there for me. He never gave a shit that he was hanging out with not only the only gay kid in town, but the only black kid, too. He was my boy from the start and I was his. Reason number two I need to end my obsession with the oldest Baxter son. They're like family to me, or at least they've always accepted me as such.

More laughter from the other side of the room. Nearly everyone at the party is congregating around Levi and he's making the holiday party all the merrier, soaking up being the center of everyone's universe.

"He's such a fucking bastard. Always has to be in the middle of everything," Chris says, each of his words making me feel guiltier and guiltier, because as much as he can't stand his brother, and as much as I love Chris, I understand the draw of Levi. There's something about him, and even after all these years, I have to grudgingly admit that it's still pulling me in, too.

***

It's a couple hours later when I'm sitting in the yard on a two-person swing. We got lucky and ended up with a few hours of sunshine—something that doesn't happen often during December in Oregon—so I'm soaking it in.

We ate a while ago. The party has thinned out a bit, and Chris went to the store with his mom. My dad isn't here. The Baxters invited him—they always do, and he always appreciates it—but he likes being alone too much. He has ever since Mom left us. He never got over losing her, and if that's what losing someone does to a guy, count me the fuck outta ever being in a serious relationship.

There's movement on the side of the house, a flash of color, and I look up and see Levi kneeling, his back against the house and his face buried in his hands.

What the hell?

It almost looks like he's rocking, like his hands are knotted in his hair. Then, just like that, he pushes to his feet, straightens out his clothes, and turns around.

His eyes land on me instantly. And then…he smiles, his body language one hundred percent different than it was a minute ago.

In long, confident strides, Levi makes his way to me, making me wonder if I misjudged what I'd seen.

He's wearing a long-sleeved shirt that hugs his chest and arms and a pair of loose jeans riding low on his hips. Dude, I love that. Love seeing the edge of a guy's boxers sticking out over his jeans and rubbing my tongue along the seam.

"How's it goin' T-Rex? Enjoying your sophomore year?" He plops down onto the seat beside me, his arm, hot and hard, brushes against mine. He doesn't move and I sure as hell don't move because he's gorgeous and I definitely don't mind a gorgeous guy touching me. I do, however, wish he didn't call me T-Rex.

"Don't call me that."

"Dinosaurs, man. That's all I have to say. You were what, ten or eleven when we met you? I think you were obsessed with dinosaurs until you were at least sixteen."

"Fuck off." But what he's said is pretty close to the truth. I used to want to be a paleontologist, which is funny considering I'm now an English major. Plus, those aren't the kind of bones I'm into anymore, but it was a good aspiration for a kid.

"Embarrassed?" he teases, his voice a little softer than it usually is.

"No. And I was fourteen when I stopped liking dinosaurs. You can give it up now." There's nothing like the object of your fantasies seeing you as nothing more than a kid who he calls T-Rex.

"Aww, but I like to call you T-Rex." Levi wraps an arm around my neck, and then pretends to ruffle my nonexistent hair. I keep it cut short enough that his attempt is impossible. And yeah, did I mention he treats me like a fucking kid?

"Get off." I shove his arm away and Levi lets me.

"I'm just giving you shit. It's good to see you."

First, if he wanted to see me, it wouldn't be hard considering he's at Stanford School of Medicine and I'm thirty miles away at San Francisco State University. And second, I wish he was thinking it's good to see me naked, but hey, I'll take what I can get. "Yeah, it's good to be home."

Levi laughs humorlessly. "If you say so."

At that, I turn to face him. That's not something I would ever expect Levi to say. Yeah, everyone's always known

Levi's too big for Coburn, but I thought he'd always loved home, too. Ever since he was a kid we all knew he'd grow up to be a big-shot doctor like his dad. Levi's the guy who has everything and everyone loves him, so I'm not sure why he would hate being back here temporarily. "What's that supposed to mean?"

He doesn't answer right away. As he runs a finger over a seam on the swing's arm, he's almost subdued—like he's a different guy than the one who was laughing and joking earlier, a different guy than the one I've always known. "Nothing. Ignore me, T-Rex. I'll catcha later, yeah?" Without waiting for me to reply, Levi gets up and walks away, and I'm still sitting here trying to figure out what in the hell happened.

11

CHAPTER TWO

"Dude, I think that guy's checking you out." Chris points
across the mall's food court. *"That one right there."*

"What the hell? Put your hand down! Don't point!"
There's a smacking sound when I swat at his hand, and then
Chris lowers it.

"He just looked again, bro. Go talk to him."

Yeah, because that's going to happen. I'm sixteen years
old and the only experience I have with boys is online or
watching porn, and I'm pretty sure neither of those count.
Plus, how do I even know if he's gay or not? *"Nah, I'm cool."*

"Toby..."

"No. Let it go, Chris." Jesus. I appreciate the effort but
things aren't the same for me as they are for him. I wouldn't
know the first thing about talking to a guy, and I sure as shit
don't have the balls just to walk up to someone when I don't
even know if they're queer or not.

*"Sorry, man, I'm just sayin'. It's not often we get to
come into Portland and since there's no one in Coburn..."*

Believe me, I get it. I'm the one who lives it. Still doesn't mean I'm going to talk to some random dude, though. It also doesn't mean there's not always this ache in my gut, embarrassment too because I'm older than Chris but he obviously has more experience than I do. I forget that sometimes, if I hadn't failed kindergarten, Chris and I probably wouldn't be friends right now.

"What time is it? Maybe you should text her again?" It's a shitty subject change, because I know Chris doesn't want to talk about Sue anymore than I want to talk about random pretty boy in the mall.

"I've texted like fifteen times. She's not coming." He looks down at his hands, and a pang hits my chest for him. "Levi's never going to stop teasing me about this. I wish Mom wouldn't have made him drive us here." We were supposed to meet a girl here that Chris has been crushing on. He asked his mom to drop us off, but she couldn't. His dad didn't have time, and my dad doesn't do stuff like that, so we were stuck with Levi since we don't have our licenses yet. "I can't believe she bailed on me."

Chris rubs his nose, making me wonder if he might cry. I've never seen him cry over something like this, but I know how bad he really wants a girlfriend. Levi probably had five at the same time at our age, and everything's always a competition when it comes to them. Or at least, Chris feels like he always has to catch up to his brother.

"If she ditched you, she's not worth your time. Fuck her."

Chris grins. "She has small tits, too."

"I wouldn't notice." I shrug and he laughs.

We're quiet for a few minutes, people-watching, when he says, "Are you sure you don't wanna try...? This doesn't have to be a bust for you. I can...like go talk to him or whatever. See if he's gay and tell him you're interested if you want."

Risking a glance, I look over at the guy. He looks our way and smiles, making my stomach drop. It's a cool-ass thing Chris is offering. Most guys wouldn't do it, but he always has my back. He's the only person in my life who really does. The guy turns, and then I do as well. I wouldn't even know what to do with him if he was interested. "Nah, that's cool. Good lookin' out, though."

"I got you." We bump fists and then Levi walks up with whatever girl he's banging this week.

"You twerps ready to go? And no girl? Aww, did my little brother get stood up? I wouldn't know what that feels like." Levi winks at Chris, and the girl on his arm giggles.

"Fuck you!" Chris shoves up from his chair and starts to walk away.

"I was kidding, man. Chill out. I'm sorry, bro!"

Levi actually sounds pretty sincere about being sorry—at least he does to me—but Chris doesn't stop walking until we get to the car. He's quiet the whole way home. I spend my time feeling bad for him and feeling like shit for me, too. I should have talked to that guy. Sue shouldn't have ditched out on Chris.

When they drop me off at home, Chris and I bump fists again. When I get in the house, I head straight to the kitchen. Dad's sitting at the table, doing a puzzle. For nearly five minutes I stand there watching him, waiting for him to realize I'm there. Wishing he'd ask me how it went and that I could

14

tell him that I don't know how to talk to boys. He might not be able to help, but at least I could talk to him about it.

But he doesn't notice I'm there. Eventually, I turn around, go to my room, and spend the rest of the evening there.

When I get home from the party at the Baxter's, I know exactly where to find my dad. "Hey, Dad, I brought you a plate."

He looks up at me from his chair in front of the TV. There's a basketball game on and I'm sure he'd rather give the game his full attention than me. Dad loves sports. He watches any and all of 'em that he can. He played a lot in school as well, from what I've been told. I played a little baseball—didn't hate it, didn't love it, it was just a thing I did. Maybe because I knew he'd like it. It gave us something to talk about, when normally we struggle for words.

"Thanks. It smells great." He reaches a hand out to me and takes the plate. His dark skin looks thin, frail, as though it would rip easily even though he's not very old. My grandmother gives him shit for not taking better care of himself. She's the only person my dad really listens to. She's a tough old lady from the South who dealt with a lot of racism growing up, but she never let it jade her. Make her tough as hell? Yes. Jaded? No.

Dad told me he was scared to bring a white woman home when he met Mom, but my grandma didn't bat an eye. It seems crazy to me that he would have to worry about that, but then I was scared to tell him I'm gay and he couldn't have cared less. Logically, I should have known he wouldn't have much of a response since he doesn't care about much of anything. It's not how he's built.

When I remember he thanked me for the food, I reply, "No problem."

"Did you have fun?" he asks.

"Yeah, it was good to see everyone." And then silence. Neither of us knows or has anything to say from here. It's not that we don't love each other in our way. He doesn't say it and doesn't show it, but I figure he has to. He stayed when Mom left–the last time when she bailed for good, and the few other times she'd disappeared in my life. He came home that night she'd ghosted, when I was scared and alone and didn't know what to do. That has to mean something. We just don't know what to say. We have nothing in common. Mom left, and then I met Chris and the Baxters let me hang out with them, so Dad and I never learned how to talk to each other. He just....let go.

"Food's good," he says after about fifteen minutes. The words carry a hint of pain in them, as though he too is thinking about how we don't know how to talk to each other.

"Yeah, it was. They always make a good meal."

My dad and I aren't big cooks. My roommate at school talks about how he misses his mom's cooking. Mine hadn't been real fond of making meals for her family.

"I'm going to go hit the shower." I stand before spouting the lie I'm about to give him because getting out of here is better than fumbling for words. "I'm meeting Chris. We're going out tonight." Since I've been away at school I've forgotten what it's like to live with my dad—a guy who I love, but who also might as well be a stranger. Sometimes I think he lives off his loneliness. He doesn't need good food or friends or company. He sure as hell doesn't need me.

"Okay, have fun." Dad gives his attention back to the TV and I make my escape. My shower is quick and then I change into my favorite jeans and a green, fitted T-shirt with a V-neck. It looks good on me. I've been told that more than once. Men seem to dig the combination of my light brown skin and green eyes. The shirt makes my eyes stand out, "pop" or some shit like that. At least that's what they say before I stick my tongue down their throats.

"See ya later," I call out as I leave. Dad mumbles a goodbye, and then I hop into my Honda and make the thirty-minute drive into Portland.

I could have called Chris and done something with him, but if I'm being honest, that's not really where my head's at tonight. My mood leaves me with two choices: Grindr or making the trip into Portland for a club. Even though I'm underage, clubbing is a possibility because this guy I met at school hooked me up with an incredibly realistic fake ID. It's never let me down.

Since it's still early, I kill a little time with a stop by a coffee shop. I fuel up on caffeine and then I'm on my way. When I get to the trendy neighborhood where the club is supposed to be, I see a line winding partway down the block. A good sign that Touch must be a pretty good place to go. I'm curious how the clubs here differ from those in the Bay Area. I haven't been able to hit any up in Oregon.

My pulse kicks up, going faster and faster the closer I get to the head of the line. I won't get caught, never have, but adrenaline always shoots through me until the second they hand the ID back and let me go inside.

Tonight the door routine goes the same as it always does. Inside feels familiar, too. The music bumping, bass making the walls vibrate, hundreds of men dancing and grinding against each other. Some talking, drinking, and, "Hey, sexy." A hand runs down my arm.

"Hey," I reply, but one look tells me he's not what I'm looking for tonight. He's thinner than me, smaller, with soft features and eyeliner. He's pretty. Really fucking pretty and I don't discriminate about shit like fem or masculine like I hear all over hook-up apps. He's just not what I want tonight... Not someone so...forward. I want to prove to myself I really made progress after leaving Coburn. Tonight, I want to go for who and what I want.

He nods and I nod back, and then I keep moving through the crowd. I didn't come here to drink so I ignore the bar altogether and make my way out to the dance floor. It's packed with people, mostly men, sweating, touching, and some kissing as I make my way through them to find a spot to dance.

Still amped up on adrenaline, letting myself thrive off the life around me, I start to move.

It's not long before sweat drips down my back I'm dancing so much. When a guy comes close, I move up against him as his arms encircle my waist and we dance. He doesn't stay, which is okay with me, because for some reason, he doesn't make my dick even stir.

It wasn't what I really came here for, the dancing, but now that I'm in the zone, I feel it in each step I take and every breath that fills my lungs. It's crazy how addicting a place like this can feel, how you can thrive on all the people moving and dancing around you.

A HUNDRED THOUSAND WORDS

"You're fucking gorgeous. You wanna get out of here?" The voice hits a switch in my brain, alerts and alarms going off. Wires cross because I can't have fucking heard who I think I just heard. Still, it's a reflex to whip around, a reflex to almost swallow my tongue, too. Somehow I manage not to choke as my vision zeroes in on the side profile of Levi Baxter. Straight Levi Baxter who just told a man he's gorgeous and asked to leave with him. As soon as my brain comes to terms with the idea I am actually looking at Levi, my next thought is to immediately wonder why in the hell he couldn't have been saying that to me.

Levi looks my way. I'm not sure he sees me because his gaze bounces to the blond he was talking to. A second later, he whips my direction again. "T-Rex?" he says and then gets this big-ass, goofy smile on his face, showing off his dimples and making me realize what must be going on here.

He's obviously fucking wasted. Maybe he stumbled into the wrong club. Not like that explains what he just said to the guy, though.

"What the hell are you doing in here?" he asks.

"Me? I'm gay. What in the hell are *you* doing in here?"

"But you're only twenty." Levi cocks a brow at me, still sloppy-smiling. Oh yeah, he's fucking gone.

"Yeah, but I like dudes—umpf." Levi stumbles into me, cutting me off before he wraps an arm around my shoulders. "It's good to see you, T-Rex. Did I tell you that earlier?"

Yes, he did, but I wouldn't mind him saying it a few hundred more times, just so I can engrave the sound into my mind.

"You're such a cool-ass kid."

19

Not the kid part, though. Scratch *kid* from his vocabulary when he's talking about me. "I'm not a kid. You're only three years older than me. And you're drunk, Levi." He leans closer to me and he smells like a mixture of alcohol, sweat and cologne. "Jesus, what the hell are you doing here? And why are you so drunk? I've never seen you like this before."

There are no doubts in my mind that Levi enjoys partying from time to time, but he's never been the sloppy drunk that he is right now. He's the kind of guy who can have a good time, party, yet still manage to ace every test and get into med school.

"I came to get laid!" he yells in my ear and yeah, I'll admit blood starts heading to my dick. He came to get laid. I came to get laid. It would make sense if we got laid together—as in the two of us, sweaty and naked as I rail him.

"But now I'm tired," he says as we head off the dance floor, "and the guy I was cruising left. My hotel is across the street. Walk with me, T-Rex. Chris's lucky to have you, have I ever told you that?" By the bar he leans toward a guy with dreads. "This is my little brother's best friend," Levi tells him, hollering over the thumping music.

The words are like a punch to the gut even though they shouldn't be. It's who I am. I'm Chris's best friend, but hell, I've known Levi long enough that I should be considered his friend, too. Brother connection aside, Chris and I were never the kind of people Levi would have hung out with.

"I don't think he cares," I tell Levi. "Come on, let's go."

His arm is still draped over my shoulder. I grab onto it and lead Levi toward the door. My mind goes a million miles an hour—questions firing off in rapid succession. He might be

20

gay...Could he be gay? He's here, that has to mean something other than straight, right?

Something's going on with Levi that I don't know about, and I'm assuming his family doesn't either because Chris would have said something to me. But this is Levi. He's not the type to hide. If he were gay, he'd say so. He knows his family wouldn't care. They've never given a shit that I'm gay.

It's like we step into a different world when we get outside. It's quieter even though there are still little clusters of people around. When Levi stumbles slightly, I wrap my arm around his waist to steady him, feel the poke of his hipbone into my hand. I'm going to fucking kill him. I can't believe he got this drunk, made his way into a gay club, and now I'm babysitting him because he can't make it to his room. Nice of him to ruin both our nights. "Which way, Jack Daniels?"

"Ha. You're funny. When'd you get so funny, T-Rex?"

I'm really not that funny. If he were sober, he wouldn't think so either. "Why are you calling me that so often? You haven't called me that on a regular basis since I was a kid."

"Don't know." He shrugs. "Feels right, I guess. Across the street. They had the right idea building their hotel across from a club."

I lead him toward the crosswalk and wonder if this is typical behavior from him since he went to college. It doesn't feel right. It doesn't feel like the Levi I know.

"You smell good... Like fucking." Levi inhales a deep breath. "Whoa, I didn't mean you smell like fucking, but it's all...soapy mixed with mint. I like it."

I let out a groan, my cock already starting to fill with blood at just the mention of smelling like sex and the fact that he thinks I smell good.

"Don't say things like that to me. Please don't." Life would really be so much easier if I didn't get hard for Levi every time I saw him. Saying things like that to me will only make things worse.

"Why?" he asks.

"Because I said."

"Make me," he tosses back and I roll my eyes at him. Levi laughs, just as the *walk* symbol lights up and I start to lead him across the street. "I'm kidding. It sounded like one of those 'Am not! Are too!' fights Chris and I get into."

I hate that he's comparing our conversation to the kind of bickering he'd do with his little brother, so I say, "You sound like a brat because you're drunk. What room are you in?" I open the hotel's door and he takes his arm out from around me to walk in. As we walk through the lobby, his arm comes back. I put my hand on his waist, feeling that bone again.

"Two thirty-seven. Seriously, what the fuck kind of soap do you use?" He inhales again, and I want him to bury his face in my neck until he can place it.

"Whatever's on sale," is what I reply, though I'm pretty sure I'll stick with this brand once I go home and figure out what it is.

We step into the elevator and we're silent as we go up. Levi's still holding me so I'm holding him.

I jump when the elevator *dings* and Levi chuckles. I roll my eyes at him, enjoying the drunk version of Levi. Not that I don't enjoy the sober Levi because I do. Despite his attitude, I've never been immune to his charm or his looks. But sober

Levi wouldn't have needed me to walk him to his hotel.

When he gets to his room, he fumbles with his key card a few times before he finally gets it to work.

He pushes the door open and steps inside, but there's not a chance I'm following. "Sleep it off," I tell him. "Text me tomorrow so I know you're okay. Shit…you don't have my number do you?" Why would he? It's not as though we spend time on the phone with each other.

"You're leaving?" His brows pull together and he gets this cute wrinkle over his nose. "Come hang out with me a bit, T-Rex. I'm not in the mood to be alone."

And he sounds almost…sad. I'm not sure I've ever heard Levi sound sad in my life.

CHAPTER THREE

We stand on either side of the door's threshold and look at each other. I'm wondering who in the hell this guy is because he's not the Levi I grew up with. The Levi I know would never be sentimental or sloppy drunk or complain about being alone. In fact, I can't think of a single time Levi has admitted a weakness to me or anyone else. He's the guy who lives out his dreams and goes for what he wants, with or without the help of others. One reason why Chris has always been jealous of Levi is because Levi has no fear and always succeeds.

I remember one time I was over at the Baxter's house for dinner. Dr. Baxter had this habit of giving Levi books on sports medicine, and at the dinner table the Doc would give Levi pop quizzes like he was one of Levi's teachers. Dr. Baxter would glow with pride when Levi got questions right, and Levi would grin, all full of smugness because no one got the best of him.

The self-important smile hadn't been there on the night I'm remembering. His dad had thrown questions at him, but

Levi had this quiver in his voice I'd never heard from him before. Like he was nervous, and that word shouldn't have a place in his life. Still, he got four of five questions right. Dr. Baxter told him how proud he was of him and Levi soaked it all in. After his dad left, Levi looked at me and Chris and said, "I almost shit my pants when he started asking me questions on that text. I haven't read the damn thing yet."

I wasn't sure why it had mattered so much to him. It was just a game between him and his dad. Who cared if he hadn't done well? That was Levi, though. He had to be perfect.

Bringing me back to the present, Levi grabs my wrist. "I said, come in." His somber tone is gone. He pulls me into the room, and I don't fight him. A feather could've knocked me into the room with him.

"Okay." I close the door behind me, and then Levi is kicking out of his shoes.

"Make yourself comfortable."

It's really hard to get comfortable when you're…well, hard. And yeah, I know, he hasn't done anything so there's no reason for me to be, but all I can think about is him saying he wants to get laid and then asking me to stay with him. It's stupid. It would be a huge mistake to bang my best friend's brother. Things would be awkward every time I was with the Baxters and Chris would kick both our asses, but I'm really not sure I'd have it in me to think straight if Levi made the offer.

He yawns, stretches. His shirt pulls up when he does, and he rubs a hand over his abs and through the light dusting of hair there. Goddamn his stomach is sexy. There's definition in his abdominal muscles—a light six-pack—but he's not one of those guys who looks like he spends his life in the gym. He's real, more lean muscle than anything else.

Real is hot.

It's obvious I don't affect him at all, because he hardly spares a glance my way as he flops onto the bed, and I carefully sit in the chair.

It's killing me, this whole fucking thing is, and I have to know, "What were you doing in that club tonight, man?"

"I'm drunk," he replies.

I know it's true, but I still don't want to hear it. I want there to be a different reason for him to have been there.

"So you were drunk and accidentally went into a gay club?"

"Didn't say that." He yawns again. "I'm tired. Are you as tired as I am?" Levi's voice gets softer as he speaks.

And I am pretty tired. Confused and horny, too. "Yeah, it's late. I should go. Are you going to be okay?" If he gets sick or something, he probably shouldn't be alone.

Fidgeting in the chair, I wait for his answer. It seems like a big deal, though I'm not really sure why.

"Yeah, I'm good. Stay, though. Like we said, it's late."

"There's only one bed. I shouldn't—"

"Turn off the light and get into the goddamned bed, Toby. Unless you have somewhere else to go."

"I don't," jumps out of my mouth. "Have somewhere else to go, I mean."

"Then get in the bed. It's big. I'm not going to jump you.

26

I just…" He rolls onto his side, his thick, dark lashes fluttering as though he can hardly keep his eyes open. "It's nice to be comfortable…to be around someone who makes me feel like Levi, whoever the hell that is."

How am I supposed to say no to that? His statement makes a hundred other questions spring to my mind. I really need to solve the puzzle created by this new Levi. "You're Levi. Who else would you be?"

"Thanks," he mumbles, closing his eyes. His hair flops over his forehead as he curls into a ball. He looks so young. I've always seen him as this huge force, older and better than me and Chris. But right now he looks…lost. "Hit the light. Come to bed."

It's fucking crazy but I'm actually shaky as I do what he says. I turn off the light, toe out of my shoes, and then lie down beside him. This isn't my first time sharing a bed with a guy, but it feels like it is.

The bed shifts and I tense up.

"T-Rex?" Levi whispers after a moment.

I let out a breath. "Yeah?"

"Did you ever realize that your life wasn't what you thought it would be?" he softly asks. "Or that you weren't who you thought you'd be? What I mean is… Did you think your life would go one way, or you'd want one thing—but then you got thrown for a loop when you realized it wasn't going to go how you thought?"

Even though my brain tells me not to, I roll onto my left side and face Levi. "Yeah." Nothing in my life is what I thought it would be. I never thought Mom would leave permanently, even though she sometimes mentally checked

27

out even when she was home. Didn't think I'd grow up to want boys instead of girls. Didn't think I'd have no idea how to talk to the man who loved me and stuck around. "Almost everything in my life has thrown me for a loop." Especially tonight.

There's a long pause that sounds like static in my ears. And then... "See? Somehow I knew you'd understand." The bed moves again, and then Levi's arm drapes over my waist. "Goodnight, T-Rex."

I'm scared to move, to breathe, to do anything that might pull me out of this moment, so instead I say the same thing I've said to him a couple times today. "Don't call me that."

"Good night, Toby."

"'Night, Levi."

And then the lucky bastard falls asleep. I stay awake half the night, still afraid that the smallest twitch will wake me up and none of this will have happened.

CHAPTER FOUR

I rolled over once, but other than that I'm not sure I moved all night. Even in my sleep my body was like...*let's just stay right here with the warm arm over me, and now the erection against my ass.* But it's morning and I really need to take a piss. I'm hard too and Levi's snoring away behind me, alcohol breath on my neck. He'll probably wake up with no memory of how I got into bed with him, and why I agreed to be here even though I was sober.

Then time speeds up like someone hitting the fast-forward button as the arm around me jerks, the bed dips, and suddenly the warmth of Levi gone. I think Levi hits the floor because I hear a thud immediately followed by, "Oh shit."

It's a reflex to roll toward his side of the bed. He stands slowly and doesn't say a word as I give him a once-over. I realize at least one of us moved during the night because he's wearing nothing except boxer briefs, the outline of an extremely prominent erection under the white material.

Levi stares. "Did we—"

"No," I interrupt him before he finishes, still looking at

his crotch.

"Thank God." The comment makes me jerk my eyes away from his package. He runs a hand through his hair, pushing it away from his face, but it falls back onto his forehead.

I shove up against the headboard. "Fuck you, man. No one's complained about me before."

The right side of Levi's mouth rises in a smile. The asshole doesn't even have a hangover by the looks of it.

"I'm sure you're great in bed, but I also think you can agree that sleeping with each other wouldn't be the best thing to do. You're like part of the family."

"Like" and "are" are two different things. I'm not related to him, and even though I'm okay with Chris feeling like I'm his brother, it rubs me raw to hear it from Levi. He touches his temples then, and I wonder if he really does have a hangover. Good, he deserves it.

"What the hell were you doing in that club last night?" Turning, I get out of bed with my back to him.

"I have a headache. Can we do this later?"

"No, because after I take a piss, I'm leaving. Hell, I didn't even plan to stay out all night. If we're being honest, you fucked up my plans. I wanted to get laid."

Levi frowns. I see my shoes by the chair and reach for them and then he's there, grabbing my arm. I look up at him and catch another glimpse of that surprising loneliness in the dark brown of his eyes.

"I was there for the same reason you were," he says.

My pulse speeds up. Levi's hand is sweaty against my arm. "You're gay?" Holy fuck. How is Levi Baxter gay and I never knew it? Why hadn't he come out?

"No." He lets go of me and shrugs. "I'm bi, though." He presses his hand to his forehead. "My fucking head's gonna explode. I need to get some caffeine and pain medicine. Have coffee with me. We can talk then."

Levi steps away but I don't move. Talk about head explosions. Levi's bisexual? The idea makes every notion I've ever had about him detonate. And who knows when the dust will settle enough for me to see how I'm supposed to deal with all this?

Levi turns back to look at me. "You okay?"

No, I'm really fucking not. I actually feel like I might get sick.

"Did I... Did I do something? Did I hit on you last night and make you uncomfortable?"

Yeah, getting hit on by him would make me uncomfortable, but probably not in the way he's thinking.

"T-Rex?"

That snaps me out of it. "Jesus Christ, if you call me that again I'm going to knock you out."

Levi's almond-shaped eyes wrinkle around the edges as though he's studying something very closely. Me, I guess. "I can handle that. Seriously, though, go have coffee with me. I owe you for babysitting my grown ass last night while I acted like a kid."

That makes me smile. If someone would have told me I'd ever run into a stumbling, sloppy-drunk Levi I would have called them a liar. "You were ridiculous."

Levi shrugs. "I have some ridiculous stories about you, too."

"From when I was a kid. You're in medical school. You're not supposed to get to have fun anymore. You're old now," I tease him, but the lighthearted banter dies somewhere between us. Levi groans and then reaches for a bag on the bedside table.

"Don't go anywhere. I need to clean up real quick."

He closes the bathroom door before I can tell him I need to take a leak. I pace around the hotel room like an idiot, partly because my bladder might explode and partly because I just found out Levi is bisexual. I'm still trying to figure out how I didn't know or how anyone at home doesn't. Maybe that's what the change in him has been, but that doesn't completely fit. He was in that club last night. He easily admitted to being bi, so I don't know why that would cause the look of sadness in him that keeps making appearances.

It's about five minutes later when the bathroom door opens. "Catch," Levi says around a toothbrush hanging out of his mouth. My fingers latch onto a second toothbrush. He's wearing pants and a hoodie now, making me wish I had taken the time to admire him half-dressed more than I had.

After I stand here like an idiot for a minute, Levi sticks his head out again. "Come brush your teeth so we can go."

"Okay." What the hell is wrong with me? I'm acting like the kid that I don't want Levi to see me as.

He finishes brushing not long after I start, and then he leaves the bathroom like…nothing. Which is all it should be. It's me who's making a big deal out of nothing. We passed out in the same bed together. End of story.

I finish brushing, close the bathroom door and take care of business. When I come out, Levi's leaning against the door to the hall with his eyes closed.

"Let's go. It's catching up with me."

We're quiet as we take the elevator down. Levi makes a quick stop in the lobby, buying a travel package of Tylenol. After leaving the hotel, he suggests we head to a little diner about three blocks away. I say, "Fine."

I hadn't taken a jacket or hoodie with me last night since I planned to be indoors the whole time. The hairs on my arms rise as goosebumps travel up my chilled skin. Finally, we step inside and there's warmth. Thank God.

"Two?" a gray-haired waitress asks. Levi nods.

She shows us to a table and leaves us with menus. I open my mouth and say the first thing that comes to mind. "Can we talk about you being bi, now?"

Levi smiles and holds up a finger. The waitress comes back, fills our cups and then walks away. "Let's order first. I need to know I have food coming before anything else."

Food, because that's what's important right now. Doesn't he realize I'm dying over the fact that he likes dick? I'm trying to hold back a barrage of visuals—mostly me pounding Levi the way I always wished I could. "Yeah, sure."

"You're pouting."

"I'm not pouting," I reply.

"Yes, you are."

"No, I'm—can we not do this? You made me argue with

you like a twelve-year-old last night, too."

Levi laughs and I have to fight myself not to do the same. There's an unexpected comfort between us that comes from years of knowing each other even though we've never been close.

"Look she's already coming back. Hurry and pick something to eat and then I can let you in on my deep, dark, secret that's really not a secret at all."

"It is to me."

Levi eyes me with a dark, questioning look that I don't understand.

He orders first when the waitress arrives, getting eggs, bacon and pancakes. From my experience, I couldn't eat shit like that when I had a hangover. Even the thought of food would make me sick. Of course, like everything else in life, hangovers seem easy for Levi.

"I'll take the same." After handing my menu to the waitress, I cross my arms and lean back in the chair, waiting for Levi to speak. He fixes up his coffee—French Vanilla creamer and sugar—before taking a drink.

"Like I said, I'm bi. I like men and women both. I'm not sure what else you want me to say."

Being gay wasn't a huge struggle for me. Not like it is with a lot of people. It didn't take me years to come out. There are no horror stories. Even though in some ways it was an unexpected turn, I never wished I was anything other than who I am. Yeah, I worried about my dad a bit, but that's all. What I did feel was really fucking alone. Again, it sucked being the only queer guy in town. I'd wanted someone like me in my life and now I find out he was right there and never told me.

"Everything. I want you to tell me everything."

CHAPTER FIVE

Levi holds up his coffee cup and takes a drink. "You're a lot bossier than you used to be."

"And you're stalling."

He grins. "It's good to see you."

This is the third time he's told me that. It makes my skin prick with a welcome heat and also confuses the hell out of me. I'm about to have breakfast with the guy who gave me and Chris shit all the time, a guy who always treated me like I was a pain in the ass. We've never done something like this, just the two of us, in our lives. "You're different. I don't get you."

He mock-rolls his cedar-colored eyes. "I'm not different and there's nothing to get."

He's lying and I have a feeling he realizes I know that.

Levi sets his cup down and leans back. When he does, he stretches his legs forward, his right leg touching me. "I never really thought about guys until I left for college. One of my frat brothers was gay. He was a senior when I was a

36

sophomore. We got pretty close that year. He became a good friend. I found myself noticing him—the way he moved, the way he smelled, the way he looked. He noticed me noticing him, and we ended up screwing around. I liked it. Really fucking liked it. It happened a few times, then he graduated and that was that with him, only I realized it wasn't just him I was attracted to. There were a few guys over the years. It doesn't change how I see women, though. I want them, too. Both sexes are beautiful to me. Sometimes I'm attracted to a woman, sometimes a man. It's as easy as that."

"Why didn't you ever say anything?" I came out my freshman year of high school, and when I did it, I came out to everyone. That's who I was and that's all there was to it. It felt like something I couldn't hide, like it was as obvious as my skin.

"Why would I tell my parents? It would be different if I was in a relationship with someone, but that never happened. It's not like I was going to call them and be like, 'Hey, I got railed by this really sexy guy last night. I thought you should know.'"

I hadn't meant his parents. I meant why didn't he ever say anything to me.

The waitress comes back with our plates then, saving me from having to reply right away. At this point, I'm not sure what I'd say, considering I'm sitting here getting my feelings hurt about something I have no right to give a shit about.

"Would you boys like anything else?" Before replying to our waitress, I glance over to see her nametag.

"I'm okay, Helen. Thanks."

As soon as she walks away, Levi says, "You've always

done that. When you'd go out to dinner with our family, I always noticed you tried to call the waiters and waitresses by their names."

It's a struggle, but I keep my eyes from finding Levi's. Discomfort starts twisting deep in my gut. Yeah, that's something I've always done, but I've never realized anyone noticed. "My mom was a waitress. I remember her telling me that it made her feel good when people called her by her name."

After salting and peppering my eggs, I take a bite. It's then that Levi finally replies. "That's nice of you…to do that." And then he shrugs.

If I'm being honest, I hadn't planned to say it. The words somehow snuck past my lips.

We eat in silence. The whole time I'm thinking again about how strange it is that I've shared meals with the Baxters for years, but that this is the first time I've eaten just with Levi. It's not until I finish eating and set my fork down that I ask the question that's been hiding in the back of my head. "Last night you said something about your life not being what you thought, or you not being who you thought… Is that about being bi? You gotta know your family won't give a shit, man."

"No." Levi shakes his head. "Hell no. And if anyone did have a problem, fuck them. I don't care about that. I never hid it at school, either. It's just…it's hard to explain…" He takes a drink of his coffee. "I think the food's helping my hangover. I feel a little better."

"Smooth transition on the subject change."

He gets this playful, cocky smile that I'm used to seeing

from him. "Thanks." Levi winks, but he can't sway me from wanting to know what's going on behind that charming as hell mask of his.

I remember the way his whisper sounded in the dark hotel room last night, the quaver in his voice. The way his arm had felt warm and heavy across my waist. My desire to know more makes me brave, braver than I usually am with Levi. "You said last night you knew I'd understand."

"I was drunk off my ass last night. Jesus, you should have heard the thoughts in my head when I woke up in bed with you. Scared me shitless. I'm so glad at least one of us was sober last night so we didn't make a really big mistake."

The statement's said offhandedly. I can tell it's not supposed to mean anything, but it's still a punch to the gut. The urge to hit him back literally tingles right beneath my skin. "You keep saying shit like that, but I'm telling you, I haven't had any complaints before." Straightening against my chair, I look around to flag our waitress over. There's no point in keeping this going. There's no reason I should be here with Levi at all. I'm Chris's friend, not his. Why should I give a shit if Levi is rejecting me, when I'm not even offering myself to him?

"It trips me out to hear you say shit like that. You're my little brother's friend. I used to hide in Chris's bedroom to scare the shit out of you guys when you'd watch horror movies." Levi laughs, but I don't hear anything funny.

"You sound like you think you're better than I am. As though you have all this life experience that I don't. You're only a few years older than me." The tingle under my skin becomes an annoying burn. I reach into my pocket for my wallet. "Here's a twenty. My food isn't more than that."

Levi pushes the money back toward me when I drop it on the table. "Put your cash away. I asked you to come with me and screwed up your night, at least I can buy you breakfast. And why are you acting all pissy? What did I do?"

"Nothing." It's not like he'd understand anyway. I'm fully aware that I'm acting like a child right now. He hasn't really done anything wrong, but I'm treating him as though he has. "Listen, I should go. This is... I don't know what this is." Levi and I aren't close friends and probably never will be. He needed help last night and I helped him. That's all there is to it, and there's no point in me sticking around and maybe getting my hopes up for more than just some weird conversation over breakfast.

As I start to push to my feet, my eyes find his. His expression isn't the cocky one he wore a few moments ago. It's more like the expression I caught a glimpse of last night—his eyes narrowing as if he's thinking hard and his lips turning down like he's not sure what he wants to say.

I'm standing there next to the table, getting ready to tell him goodbye when he says, "I heard you once, when we were younger. It wasn't long after you started spending time at our place. Your mom had left not long before. It was late and you were staying with Chris. I got up to take a piss and you were crying in the bathroom."

What the actual fuck? Telling me he heard me crying in the john when I was a kid isn't going to make this any less awkward. "Yeah, okay. Thanks for bringing that up."

When I try to walk away, Levi's warm hand wraps around my wrist. His skin isn't as clammy as it was earlier.

"I get it. Your whole life had just fallen apart. You felt

alone, lost. I guess I feel the same way sometimes. Only I don't have a real reason for it. Not the way you did."

His words bounce around in my chest, colliding with my heart. There's a quiet pain in his voice, something that's maybe been there for a while, but he's done a good job at hiding it. Right now he's not trying, he's naked and not in the way I've fantasized about too many times over the years.

"I don't know what in the fuck I'm saying." Levi lets go. "There's nothing wrong with me. I'm happy. I'm fucking lucky. I'm getting my dream. I'm going to be a goddamned doctor. I'm just..." He shakes his head. "Fuck, I don't know what I'm being. You can ignore me. I'll catcha later, T-Rex."

There's no possibility of me ignoring or forgetting what he's just said, the way he said it or how it feels. I'm standing here looking down at a guy I've known forever and feeling like maybe I don't really know him at all.

"You don't get off that easy," I tell him. "You never let me or Chris off easy and I'll be damned if I do it to you."

CHAPTER SIX

Levi leans back, staring up at me. "Think you're a tough guy now, huh?"

He's teasing me, but I'm not letting go of this sudden burst of confidence I have where Levi is concerned. "Or you're just noticing." I nod toward the door. "Let's go for a walk or something."

It takes a moment, but then Levi stands, tosses some money on the table, and follows me out of the diner. He squints as we stand on the sidewalk, making me wonder if he feels worse than he's letting on. It's dreary and grey, more like Oregon weather than the brief tease of cool sunshine from yesterday. I wouldn't be surprised if it rained soon.

"Had to want to go on a walk when I'm hungover, huh?"

"It's payback for being drunk and cockblocking me last night." We make our way down the sidewalk and now that we're out here, I'm not sure what to say. I guess I hoped that Levi would suddenly spill details from the last four and a half years of his life to me so I could understand him better, but he doesn't.

"How's school going for you?" he asks.

"Good. I've seen and done more shit in the year and a half I've been at school than I did my whole life."

Levi chuckles, this rich, husky laugh. "I hear ya. You realize there's a whole other world out there. Portland isn't even that far from Coburn, but it's still different than home. I loved Southern California. It never fucking rains there. I don't know what made me choose to go up north for med school." Another laugh.

"You sound like it's good to be home one second, and not the next." I've always felt the need to get away from Oregon and I assumed Levi felt that way, too. Leaving home seemed like it fit with all his plans—go to school, become a doctor like his dad, and own the world. That's Levi.

He sighs as we keep walking. "What's with you? Asking all the hard questions."

"Didn't know it was hard. Plus, that's not really a question. More of a statement."

"True." Levi takes a deep breath and I swear I see the wheels turning in his head. He's trying to sort through his thoughts so I hold back on asking him more questions, giving him time.

As we amble down the street, heading for a green space that looks like it might be a park, he says, "If you're expecting some big story, you're not going to get it. Like I said in the diner, there's nothing much to say. College was mostly great. I had a blast, but… Hell, I guess it wasn't what I thought it would be, either. This sounds like a lame-ass excuse, but I've always been used to things coming easy for me. Suddenly, I had to work harder than I ever had. Which is cool, I don't mind the work. Love it in a way because it's important to me to succeed, but it was different. It just…affected me in ways I never expected."

"So? You got on track." There's nothing wrong with needing a little help, but I can see it being a problem for Levi. He's always been so proud, always kept himself on a pedestal. It's why he comes off as a dickhead sometimes.

He sighs. "Yeah… I did but…shit."

"What is it?" I ask when he stalls, but then add, "Nevermind. You don't have to say anything." Hell, I don't like telling people my business. I'm not going to push someone else.

We reach the end of the block. The green space is a park, but it's a city park. Just a couple benches and some big stone planters that seem damn gray today, but probably look great in the spring and summer. We sit on one of the benches and don't speak for a few minutes. Levi raises his arms, locks his fingers together behind his head, brows furrowed. There's a million things going on in his head. I see the words scrolling across him even though they're too blurry for me to read.

"Can I tell you something?" he asks. "Something I've never even said out loud? Hell, I'm not sure why I'm saying it now but it's fucking eating away at my insides." His voice is raw pain and confusion, chaos hiding behind his soft words.

Dread scurries down my spine like a spider hurrying across the ground. Whatever he's thinking must be dire if he suddenly wants someone like me for a confidant. "Yeah. For sure. Whatever you need to say."

Levi drops his hands, a whoosh of air slides across my skin when he does. "It's going to sound ridiculous. Like I'm a fucking pussy worrying about things that shouldn't matter."

"Dude, almost everything that affects one person is a non-issue for someone else. It's your life and it matters to you. That's the only thing that's important."

"Yeah?" The wrinkle above his eyes grows deeper as though he sincerely needs me to cement the statement for him. Like he needs someone to tell him it's okay for him to be feeling whatever the hell it is he's feeling. I'm still trying to make it all compute. It's like my brain keeps crashing every time I try to make sense of the guy who always has the answers suddenly seeming lost.

"Yeah...what is it, Levi? I'm good for it. It's between us." Those words are strange to say to him.

He lets out a deep breath and then says, "I don't know if I want to be a doctor, man."

That's it? I don't know what I expected him to say, but that's definitely not it. Even when I was a knobby-kneed kid with ashy legs playing in his backyard I've always seen Levi like Dr. Baxter in so many ways—smart and confident, sure about everything he did. It was family knowledge that Levi would grow up and become a doctor like his dad. "You've always wanted to be a doctor," I blurt. I can't think of anything else to say.

"Yeah... I know I have. But then again—have I really? I don't even fucking know. I mean, I think it's always what I've wanted. But sometimes I think—do I want it just because it's what was expected?"

Holy fuck. I'm struck dumb trying to piece together what he's saying. Before I can figure out how to respond, Levi continues.

"I was at the top of my class, Toby. I used to study this shit just to impress my dad with how much I knew. It's like...hell, like sports I guess, practicing and conditioning for the season. Every box I needed to check, I checked it—extracurricular, grades, I excelled at everything. At first college wasn't what I expected it to be, but I worked that out, too. It's who I am. I don't let anything beat me. But this? This doubt is fucking beating me. I'm in my second year of Stanford School of Medicine, just like my dad, and all I can think is...what the fuck did I do? It's there, clawing at me all the damn time—the questions, my future, and then I sort of freak out and it makes me just want to fucking disappear. Then I feel like an ass for thinking that way." He nudges my elbow with his. "See? I told you not to expect something big. I'm being a pussy. That's about it."

I don't agree with him—what he's saying is a big deal. Being angry at his feelings of doubt is true to who Levi is, I think. Yet I've always admired how sure he's seemed about everything in life, and so it's hard to fit together all the pieces he's giving me so they're not just a cluster-fuck in my head. "It's your life, man. Being a doctor...that's serious shit. It's not something to take lightly."

"I've always felt like a future in medicine was this adventure I couldn't wait to live. I was going to save lives like my dad. I was going to matter. What I did would mean something. Now it's this heavy fucking weight in my chest. I'll be responsible for people's *lives*, Toby. I can't breathe thinking about it sometimes. I worked my ass off to get to where I am, and my parents paid a shit-ton of money for it. Part of me can't let med school beat me. I don't back down for shit, but then winning means my whole damn life is going to be this heavy burden on my soul that makes me feel like

I'm losing control."

I have no idea what to say to him, how to find the right words or how to string them together in a way that could help him.

This whole thing is so typical of Levi, it kind of makes me want to laugh. He's being upfront about his issues in a way I never could. It's almost as though in this moment, he's somehow secure in his insecurity, if that makes sense. "I don't know, man. I just...it's not about winning and losing. It's not about letting med school *beat* you. And even if it was, normal people aren't good at everything. It's okay to not be the best. But then you've always hated not being the best."

"Who doesn't?" he asks. I guess he has me there.

Levi drops his head back and looks at the sky. There's a purple vein running the length of his neck. A tick in his jaw indicating he's working the muscles there. "I don't know what I want, Toby. I fucking don't, and that's never happened to me. I don't think I want to wear that white coat, to be my dad, even though I respect the hell out of him. The thought makes me feel like I'm choking, like there's this hand around my throat that keeps squeezing tighter and tighter. The longer it goes, the harder it gets, but then if I don't keep going, what do I do? Does that make sense?"

I don't know what to say to him. I haven't experienced what he's saying but I can see how it could happen. But then, I think about myself, my life, and I think maybe I have experienced something similar.

He nudges my arm and we get up and start to walk again.

My gut instinct is to clam up, to lockdown, because this heart-to-heart stuff is so out of my realm of reality. I might as well be in Mordor right now. But then, he's standing here, reaching out to *me,* Toby Jackson, when he's kept this trapped inside for what sounds like years. Levi, not just anyone, Levi Baxter, and damned if I can fight the urge to find something to say to him. "When my mom left, my world was turned upside down, and I felt like I had no control. After that, I wanted control of every aspect of my life, because then if something got fucked up it was on me. No one else could cause me that kind of stress. I think it's the opposite for you. You've always had control, and known what you wanted. You've always *had* what you want and now you feel like that control is taken away. You can't control something when you don't know exactly what it is that you want."

There's a pause in conversation. Our arms brush against each other as we move in unison, almost like we're attached.

"That's the first time you've ever really said something about your mom leaving."

"I know." I'm not sure what he expects me to say beyond that. Yeah, my mom was a little spaced out sometimes. She'd get a hair up her ass and leave. One of those times she didn't come back. The end.

Maybe he can tell how hard my jaw is clenched, how hard my teeth are grinding together, because he doesn't wait for me to say anything more. He asks, "Who doesn't want med school? But, sometimes I think I'd rather do anything other than that. It's screwing with my head."

There's a part of me that feels like I'm stabbing Chris in the back by being here with Levi and listening to him share these feelings with me. But I'm honored at the same time. For Levi to trust me like this. That's something I should probably tell him, but I don't.

"They love you. They'll want you happy. You gotta know that." They might freak out a little, but I know his parents. They love Chris and Levi too much not to accept it.

Levi stops and I realize we're back at his hotel. He backs up, leaning against the building, so I move closer to him. I feel like an asshole because suddenly all I can think of is how gorgeous he is, and the way he felt against me last night. His Adam's apple bobs when he swallows. The muscles in his neck move. His eyes dart around, taking the world in the way he always does, looking for the next adventure. His hair looks soft, the way it falls on his forehead, blowing in the wind and getting into his eyes.

I want him. I've always wanted him, but before it's always seemed like a fantasy. Now—just like my perception of Levi as a person—my feelings are shifting, becoming deeper. My attraction has changed to a constant buzz, this charged energy beneath my skin. Being this close to him is making my insides go haywire.

"You're looking at me like you've never seen me before. What's up with that?" he asks, a playful tone in his voice. It's another mask, I think, the same as yesterday at the party.

"Don't know." I turn away because the last thing he needs to deal with right now is my juvenile crush on him.

"Thank you," Levi says.

"For what?"

He shrugs. "Everything, I guess. Last night. Breakfast. Listening to me ramble about shit that really doesn't matter. Telling me you get it, even if you don't."

Levi leans forward and gives me this half-hug, patting my back. It's a bro hug, not a *bone me* hug.

"I should let you get home." He pulls away. "I'm sure you're busy. I've kept you long enough. See ya around sometime, T-Rex." And then Levi walks away, and I'm standing here wondering what in the hell happened these last twelve hours.

CHAPTER SEVEN

"Mornin'," Dad says when he walks into the kitchen the next day.

He runs a hand over his head. Some of the short, dark curls in his hair are turning gray. Those gray hairs weren't there when I was home last summer.

"Hey."

He fixes a cup of coffee and I head over to the fridge to see what there is to eat. It's pretty empty like it always is, but there are eggs and cheese so I ask, "Do you want an omelet? I'm starved."

"No, that's okay. Thank you." He adds cream to his coffee, no sugar the same as he always has. It's almost as though I expected him to change while I was gone. I know I did.

"You sure?" I ask. When I was a kid, I'd make Dad omelets on Father's Day. It was one of our only traditions. It's not Father's Day, but I haven't done it in too long, so I kind of want to.

Christmas is in a few days, so maybe that's why I'm thinking about traditions. Or maybe I've been thinking about how we don't have any traditions. Like this year once again we don't have a tree. We stopped decorating one when I turned sixteen, but never really spoke about why. It's just something that happened. We kept meaning to put it up, but he was busy with work or tired and we didn't... The next year neither of us even brought it up.

"Yeah, I'm good. It was a long day at work yesterday. I think I'm going to take my coffee into the living room and watch the news."

Surprise, surprise. "Okay."

He again rubs a hand over his short hair. I jerk my hand down when I realize I'm rubbing my head, too. Subconsciously doing the same thing as my dad gives me a twist in my gut.

"You can bring your breakfast in the living room and eat—"

He only gets half the sentence out before I'm shaking my head. Closing the fridge, I say, "Nah, that's okay. I think I'm going to head over and see what Chris is up to." *Because it makes my skin feel too tight being in this house.* Which isn't fair, but it's true.

"Sounds good." Dad blows into his cup before moving toward the other room. "Have fun."

Shitty as it is, he almost sounds relieved, and in a way, I am as well.

***

The truth is, I won't go to Chris's. Even though Chris

52

would be cool with me stopping in, it would make me feel weird to show up there unannounced at breakfast time. They only get a few weeks home for the holiday. They can't want me there interrupting their family time.

It's chilly out, but not as bad as it could be. And it's not raining so that's a plus. As soon as I close the door to my car, my cell rings and I pull it out of my pocket. It's an Oregon number, but I don't recognize it. "Hello?"

"Hey. It's Levi. What's going on?"

I'm not quite sure how he got my phone number but I don't ask. "Nothing. Sitting in my car, actually. I was going to get out of the house for a bit."

There's a pause and then, "Want some company? I need to do the same thing."

There's no thought in my answer. I just open my mouth and say, "Yeah." I almost ask him if he wants me to swing by and pick him up, but that might cause problems if Chris or his parents see me. What reason would I have to explain why I'm hanging out with Levi? "Where do you want to meet?"

He lets out a deep breath. "Thank God. I thought you were going to want to come this way."

Yeah, I'd just been thinking the same thing, but it still rubs me the wrong way to hear him say it. "Because we wouldn't want anyone to know we're hanging out," I say, my tone dripping with smartass. Dude, what's wrong with me? I'm getting my feelings hurt for no reason.

"I'm not embarrassed to hang out with you. I just…fuck, I don't know, Toby. This is weird."

He's right. It is weird. I don't know what I'd been

53

thinking when I'd made that remark. "I'm giving you shit. I get it."

"Fucker. You made me feel bad when you probably feel the same way I do. Chris is protective over you." Chris is protective over anyone when it comes to Levi, but I don't tell him that. "Hang tight. I'll come over and pick you up real quick." Levi hangs up without another word.

I don't get out of my car as I wait for him. This is strange, sitting around waiting for Levi to come and pick me up, but I have a feeling it's something a lot of people have done...wait for Levi.

I let my eyes fall closed as I lean back, and my brain starts sifting through memories, a slideshow flashing across my closed eyelids.

"Can you believe Bridget fucking Maloney's been wanting to hang out with me?" Chris asks me. "I don't give a shit why it happened all of a sudden, but I'm glad. She's gorgeous. Older girls are hot." She's only a year ahead so I'm not really sure she qualifies as "older."

My shoulders automatically rise and fall in reflex. "She's aight." I wink at Chris who shakes his head at me. Chris's eyes get soft, and I know exactly where this is going before he says anything. "Shut the fuck up."

"I feel bad. I'm always talking about getting girls around you."

And he is but we're teenagers, so who gives a shit? If I had all the options he did, I'd be doing the same thing. But it's cool that he cares. That's my favorite thing about Chris. He's loyal as hell to me. He wants me around. He would

54

never leave. "You're my boy. You can talk to me about whatever you want." But there's a part of me who wishes these conversations weren't always so one-sided. "As long as there's no details." I wink at him again as we walk to his front door.

"I think I'm going to invite her over tonight since my parents will be gone. Maybe I can get Levi to get out of the house. I wish it wasn't his break."

The door opens before we can go inside. Speak of the devil, Levi steps out dressed up like he's going on a date. Inhaling, I smell his cologne, my eyes raking down his body, but then my cheeks warm and I turn away. I really shouldn't want him so much.

"Are you going to be gone tonight?" Chris asks him.

"Yep. I'm taking Bridget out. Thanks for the hookup, man." Levi smiles, and it almost looks genuine. His voice as well like he's really thanking Chris for something instead of just being an asshole. But then, is this really something that can be misinterpreted?

Levi pats Chris on the chest in what looks like another form of thanks, then jogs down the walkway, jumps into his car and he's gone.

Fuck. My stomach is somewhere at my feet. Chris is going to lose his shit, and rightfully so. Betrayal sears my gut because I was sitting here thinking about doing dirty things to Levi while he was apparently stabbing his brother in the back.

"I fucking hate him, man." Without another word, Chris walks into the house and I realize what a shitty friend I am to him, because I should hate Levi, too.

Back in the present, I hear a *knock-knock* against the window. My eyes jerk open and I scramble to sit upright. Levi's standing at the window wearing a long-sleeved shirt and jeans. He rubs his right arm with his left hand as though he's cold and trying to warm up. If I didn't know any better, I'd say he's nervous.

If I had any sense, I'd stay in this car, drive over to the Baxter's house and hang out with Chris and leave Levi alone.

Obviously, I'm a fucking idiot, because instead I push open the door and say, "All you're missing is the flowers."

What a dumbass thing to say.

"Huh?" He wrinkles his nose, and then I see the light click on in his brain. "This isn't…I didn't…"

A laugh tumbles out of my mouth and then Levi gives me a shrug. "Fucker. Let's go before I kick your ass."

Because it would obviously be a travesty for the two of us to be on a date together. *Yeah…yeah it would.* "Your car or mine?" I ask.

"Mine."

"Where we going?"

Levi shrugs. "I don't know. I haven't done any of my Christmas shopping yet. Does that sound good to you? We can hit up the mall in Portland."

"Works for me." We jump into his truck and take off. The ride's mostly quiet, just the obnoxious rumble of his engine going down the freeway. About ten minutes into it Levi asks me if I have a music preference. I like older shit— music from the nineties—but figure he doesn't have any of that so answer with, "Nah, I'm good."

He hits the radio, which is filled with crap as always. About forty minutes later we're pulling into the parking lot of the mall.

"Any idea where you want to go?" he asks.

"The only people I have to buy for are my dad and Chris. I already got Chris's gift and I have no fucking idea what to get my dad."

The corners of Levi's eyes wrinkle again and I realize they do that a lot. "Really?" We step inside the mall. It's an overload of Christmas shit and I immediately want to turn around and walk out again.

"Really what?"

"Really all of it. Just Chris and your dad? And how do you not know what to get him?"

"Because I don't really know him. Or maybe because he doesn't really like anything. He works and watches ESPN. That's about it."

Levi frowns and I see it there in his eyes. The pity. I don't want that from him or anyone else. He doesn't say anything though, just pushes up his shirtsleeves and I notice his arms are dotted with freckles, which is really fucking sexy. And that he's pale as hell. "Holy shit, you're really white. I never noticed before."

Levi laughs, but he's still watching me like he's trying to figure something out. "Hey, I've never had any complaints about my body before. Not all of us can be blessed with—"

"If you compare my skin color to food or a drink I'm beating your ass."

We squeeze through a crowd of people as we make our

way through the main court. "Huh? People do that?"

"All the fucking time. It's annoying—creamed coffee, caramel, chocolate sundae." The last one I'm making up, but still.

"With a cherry on top?" Levi winks and a slight heat forms in my lower stomach.

"Nope, no cherries here. I'm all man."

He rolls his eyes. "You're a dirty boy, Toby. Who would have thought?" We head down the main walkway before he adds, "Anyway, I wasn't going to call you a food. No worries there."

My brain tells me to keep my mouth shut, but I really don't want to listen to the warning. "What were you going to say, then? How would you describe me, because I have to tell you, I haven't had any complaints either."

Levi spares me a quick glance. He bumps into someone—the mall is crowded as hell with Christmas shoppers—and excuses himself before he says, "Check you out. Went off to college and came back a tattooed flirt. Are you looking for compliments?"

Yes, yes I am. And I have one owl on my arm. A regular inked-up motherfucker. *Right.* "I'm not looking for anything. It was just a question."

"Hmm…" He taps the side of his forehead as though he's pretending to think. Jingle Bells is playing over the mall's sound system. I hate that song. Christmas music is my downfall this time of year. "I don't think I'll tell you."

"What?" I laugh. "That's not fair." Because I really do want to know what Levi thinks of me. I want to know what kind of men he's into as well.

"Hey! I don't see you giving me any compliments. You're not gonna tell me how you see me, then I'm not doing the same for you."

Oh. Yeah…he's got me there. Not so sure I should tell him what I see when I look at him. It might make things a little awkward if he knows thinking about him gets me hard. "Eh, I guess you're right."

This time it's Levi who laughs. He has this totally unique sound to his voice—a sexy, scratchy, husky tone that's gritty as sandpaper and sounds masculine as hell.

"Now wait a minute. You had me all ready to hear what you think about me. I mean, besides *pale* that is. Christ, now I'm going to be insecure about my skin tone. Should I hit up a tanning salon today?"

Scoffing, I push my hands into my pocket. "Yeah right, insecure my ass. You forget, I know you. I was at your house every weekend when I was a kid. You had a different girlfriend every time. Chris used to talk about how much he couldn't wait to *score* like you always did. I'm pretty sure you don't get insecure about your looks. Everyone wanted you." And they had.

"That's not true, T-Rex." His voice sobers. "Things aren't always what they seem. And even if they seemed good back home, I got a hell of a wakeup call in college. It's a lot harder to stand out in the rest of the world than it is in Coburn." He shrugs. "It took me a bit to find my footing. And I got turned down plenty by both women and men." He glances at me and cocks a brow. I really, really don't need him to remind me that he's into men. That's just going to get me into a whole hell of a lot of trouble. "But yeah, maybe it's not a good idea for us to continue this conversation."

Wait. Why is that? He can't leave off on that. There has to be a reason and wishful thinking or not, the only one I can come up with is the fact that he's nervous about sexual tension between us. Which is there, at least on my end. It wouldn't bother me if it were there on his as well. When I open my mouth to tell him I changed my mind, that I'll tell him what I think about him if he tells me what he thinks about me, Levi speaks before I can. "You frown when I call you T-Rex. You asked me not to call you that—which I try not to, by the way. It comes automatic—why does it bother you now though?"

This is one thing I can't help but be honest with him about. "Because you called me that when I was a kid. I'm not a kid anymore, Levi, and I want you to know it."

He doesn't reply, just looks around me, the store at my back suddenly becoming extremely interesting. "I want to make a stop in here real quick."

CHAPTER EIGHT

"You think Chris is serious about Gemma?" Levi asks as I follow him through the store.

"Yeah. He attached the ball and chain himself the second he saw her. He called me about two weeks into the school year and said he met his dream girl. They've been together ever since." I know it's only been a few months, but there's something different about the way he talks about her. Plus, she's flying out to spend part of the break to meet his family. That has to mean something.

"No shit?" Levi chuckles. "I wonder why he didn't call and tell me."

His words make me stumble. Is he serious? Chris doesn't talk to Levi about anything, not really. He doesn't trust his brother. Levi has to know that. "He probably thought you would be too busy or something," I lie, because if Levi doesn't know, I definitely don't want to be the one to break it to him.

"Nah, he's my brother. Would have given him shit, but wouldn't have been too busy."

I'm not sure Levi would have said that a few years ago. It's strange how someone can go away and come back a different person, like the outside world has this magic power to change the things your hometown engraved into you. In a lot of ways, I'm a different person, and Levi seems to be as well.

"It'll be cool to meet her. I'm proud of him. Seems like he's doing real well."

Guilt creeps around inside me, peeking out of hiding places I didn't even know were there. Levi has no fucking clue how Chris feels about him. They're brothers. That's how brothers are supposed to relate, right? It's not as though I have experience to draw from, but listening to Levi I realize he feels a closeness to Chris that Chris isn't aware of. Because mostly all Levi does is give him a hard time. It makes me wonder if maybe we didn't really see the whole truth though. If part of it was typical brother stuff and Chris and I just saw it as Levi being a jerk or if there's more to the story. If maybe Levi didn't have little masks in place even back then the way he does now. "You should tell him. I think he'd like to hear that."

He stops at a display and I study him, wondering if I ever really knew him. It's hard to tell. He laughs the same and teases the same, but then he says things like he just did about Chris, or I think about everything from yesterday, and it's as though I'm looking at a stranger.

"Stop staring at me. You're going to make me think you want me." Levi nudges me, a smile in his voice.

"You wish," I toss back, and then we move on from the display and fall into silence.

"So what about you?" Levi asks after a few minutes.

"What about me what?"

"You didn't get serious with any guys while you were away?"

A laugh jumps out of my mouth. "Definitely not. Which is cool. I wasn't looking to. I just…" I'm just not sure if I should talk to him about this.

"Just what? Don't get shy on me now. Hey, watch out." He grabs my arm and pulls me closer. My head narrowly misses the arm on a mannequin. "You're not allowed to get hurt while we're here. I fucked up your night at the club. If something goes bad today I'll think I'm bad luck." He lets go of my arm.

"You didn't fuck up my night."

Levi's brows pull together like I've confused him. Can't blame him for feeling that way because he did, for real, mess up my plans at the club. But I can't call the night a complete waste because I'd appreciated getting insight into Levi.

"Anyway, what were you going to say?" he asks.

It's hard to explain my attitude about getting to know guys in college. Levi had such a different experience from me while growing up in Coburn, I'm not sure he'd understand. "Getting serious was the last thing on my mind," I tell him. "I basically just wanted to screw…or get head. I'm not picky. Either works for me."

Levi lets out a loud laugh, almost sounding surprised by what I said. "It's going to take me a while to get used to hearing you say shit like that, but yeah, I get it. Hell, I had plenty of girls to choose from at home, but I still felt the same way when I left."

I try to add up everything I've learned about Levi since getting home, but the results don't make sense. One minute I can understand the insecurities he's described, but the next minute all I can see is the old, confident Levi.

When he doesn't offer more of an explanation, I don't ask. We make our way around the store and Levi buys a gift for his mom before we head to a store that sells gag gifts and graphic T-shirts. He picks out a shirt with a joke about being a doctor and bedside manner for his dad. Dr. Baxter will never wear it. It's much too casual for him, but I think he'll get a kick out of it.

"You hungry?" he asks. "We can head to the food court."

"Sure, I could eat, but this place is Christmas-movie overload. Can we grab something else?"

He shrugs. "Yep. No shopping for you?"

"Nah, I'm good." We make our way back to the car before hitting up a burger drive thru and sitting in his truck to eat.

"I had a peanut butter and jelly sandwich for breakfast. I'm fucking starved." He takes a bite of his burger and then wipes a dab of ketchup from the corner of his mouth.

"Grape jelly?" It's a good question. If he answers anything other than grape, I'll realize Levi and I can never be and get over this fucked-up crush I have on him.

"Is there any other kind?"

Oh shit, I'm screwed. He loves grape jelly. There's no going back now. I cover a smile by taking a big bite of my burger. "I don't know why it's always been my favorite."

Actually, I do, but it's not something he really needs to know.

"Because it's good. It's my favorite, too."

From there we pretty much just stuff our faces. Levi shoves our burger wrappers into the bag and leans back, resting his head against the seat. "So what do you have planned for the rest of break?"

"Jack shit." I trace the lines on the truck's center console with my finger. "There's nothing here for me to do."

Levi nudges me. "What do you mean by that?"

"I don't know. It's not important." It's not like I'm going to tell him my dad and I don't spend time together and the Baxters are the only local family I have. "I'll hang out with Chris, but he has Gemma coming. Maybe I'll meet up with a few other friends if they're in town but, if we're being realistic, I'll probably just talk to guys on Grindr all day." I shrug. Chris is the only person I've kept in touch with since leaving for college.

From the corner of my eye, I see Levi turn his head toward me. I can't help but look over at him, too. "I used to wonder if you and Chris had something going on. Remember when I got suspended for that fight in high school?"

I do remember. It was the only time Levi had been in serious trouble at school. He couldn't play in one of his football games because he got suspended for that fight. "Yeah," I tell him.

"Landon was talking shit about you guys. Saying stuff he had no business saying. I always fucking hated him anyway, but the way he was saying it… Like who gave a fuck if you and my brother were together? That shit pisses me off."

Levi turns his head away, but I keep looking at him. There's a little scar by his eyebrow, but I don't know how he got it. His nose is thin, not too thin, but it's on the smaller side. It's suddenly become necessary that I memorize everything about him. Like notes I have to study for a major test, and I'm getting in my last cramming session. "Why didn't you say anything?" All we'd known was he got into a fight, not the why of it. Not that it had been in defense of Chris and me. His parents had lost their minds at the idea of Levi fighting. I can guarantee they would have changed their tune if they knew Levi was sticking up for Chris, but he never said a word.

"I didn't want you guys to know… If you were fucking around, I didn't want it to cause problems." He pauses and I wonder why in the hell Levi never showed this side of himself before now. The fact that he cares. If he had, maybe things wouldn't be so strained with him and Chris. Not for the first time it makes me want to reevaluate some of the instances from the past. If he got in that fight to stick up for us and we didn't know it, maybe he'd had reasons for some of his other behavior as well.

"Were you…? Did you ever…?" He doesn't finish his sentence.

"What?" I can't believe he even asked that. "No. Hell no. Chris is my best friend. That's all he'll ever be."

"Good." Levi closes his eyes, just closes his fucking eyes like he's going to take a nap or something, as though he didn't make it sound like he gave a shit if I was with his brother or not.

Why? Why the fuck is it good that I never had a thing with Chris? "He's straight as straight can be. Jesus, I thought I

66

would lose my mind he talked about girls so much. I love him, but not like that. I know he took shit for being good friends with me. Not all the time and not from everyone, but sometimes."

He'd been a dream friend to a kid like me. Hell, he even took me to prom. It had been a blow to the fucking ego, and I sure as hell didn't want to say yes when he asked me, but Chris said he'd rather go with his best friend than anyone else. And we both knew I didn't have any other options. Yeah, he got shit for being close with me. Not many guys would have stuck by my side.

"He's a good guy, like you. I always wondered. I could see you with someone like Chris."

It would never happen. Even if Chris was gay or bi, he's my friend. Like my brother. I could never risk losing Chris with something as temporary as a fling, or even a relationship. People pretend those last but they rarely do.

I don't really know how to respond, so I go back to what we were talking about a few minutes ago, plans for while we're home. "They're playing *Dr. Jekyll and Mr. Hyde* at the theater. I might go see that."

Levi keeps his eyes closed but his nose wrinkles. "Really? You're into that stuff?"

"Yeah. I'm not into dinosaurs anymore."

"What else are you into?"

It should be an easier question to answer than it is. "I don't know. I read. I like going to watch plays. I'm an English major."

This time he opens his eyes and turns toward me again.

"No shit?"

"Yeah, no shit. You might like going to see a play every now and then, too. I love words. Love the way people put them together. It's the most incredible form of art, if you ask me." When I realize I've gone off on a tangent, I turn and stretch just for something to do. I don't know why I just told him all of that. Like he cares.

"Can I go with you?" he asks.

I feel his eyes on me, and I roll mine. "You don't want to go. It's cool."

"Oh, and you know what I want and don't want? Can you tell me what in the fuck I want to do with my life, since I don't want to be a doctor anymore?"

"I didn't mean…" I turn his way so quickly, there's a little pinch in my neck.

"I know." He nudges my arm. "I'm going to go with you whether you like it or not. Hell, maybe I'll like *Dr. Jekyll and Mr. Hyde*. You never know."

"Okay." I'm close enough now that I can see the scar by his eye in more detail. It's in the shape of a crescent moon. The urge to lick it is there. To let my mouth trail down his face and eat at his lips. The guy is too fucking sexy for his own good.

"Okay to what? That you don't care if I go with you, or you think I might like it?"

"Both." Okay to everything right now.

We're close, too fucking close to be staring at each other like this. I'm not clear on how it happened, but I don't care either. I feel his warm breath on my face and see that there's a little spot of lighter brown in one of his eyes. I should just fucking kiss him. If it were any other guy I would have.

"Thank you," he says, his voice laced with sex. It's the voice he uses when he's with someone. Somehow I know that.

And then his hand is touching my face. He cups my cheek before sliding his hand around to rest on the back of my neck. His touch sears my skin in the best possible way. My whole body heats and then Levi gives my neck a gentle tug. So fucking gentle that I almost don't know if he did it or if I'm just moving toward him.

Our lips touch, his hair brushes my forehead and then his tongue is at my lips. *Fuck yes.* All I can think is *fuck yes*, as I open my mouth and his tongue pushes inside. Levi leans forward, closer, deepening the kiss. Levi fucking Baxter. I'm kissing Levi Baxter. My tongue is moving with his. I moan into his mouth and then he moans into mine. My dick is hard and aching as I reach up to grab his hair, to pull him closer and kiss him deeper, but as soon as I touch him, he jerks away.

"Fuck. I'm sorry." He leans against the door like he has to be as far away from me as possible. "Jesus, I can't believe I just did that. I shouldn't have kissed you, T-Rex."

Just like that, my dick goes soft. My skin burns hot for a different reason now. Why in the fuck shouldn't he kiss me? What the hell is so wrong with it?

"Yeah. Fine. No worries." I get as close to my door as I can, too. It's ridiculous and we're acting like kids. I've done more with guys I met on an app, so I'm not sure what the big deal about a kiss is. "Come on. We should get out of here."

"T—"

"Shut the fuck up. It's fine. Let's go. I'm getting tired anyway." But I'm not, not really. Apologizing for a kiss that's returned isn't something anyone should ever do. Even if he doesn't want to do it again, oh well. I just don't want to hear about how he's sorry and how he shouldn't have done it. Oh, and then hear him call me the name I've asked him not to call me too many times to count.

"Alright."

Levi's truck rumbles to a start. I've always fucking hated trucks like this—monsters driven by guys who seem like they have to make up for something with an oversized vehicle.

We're quiet as we start the drive back to Coburn. I'm pouting, but right now I really don't care.

"T-Rex…"

I squeeze my hands into tight fists, and take a deep breath so I don't lose my cool. "I swear to God if you call me that again I'm going to kick your ass."

Levi doesn't reply. We don't say anything else to each other until we get home. When we pull up to my house, it's Levi who speaks. "Gimme a call about the play thing. Shit, you don't have my number. Oh, never mind. I called you this morning. Save it."

There's a brief second where I consider going with the idea we'll actually hit up a play together. He's trying despite the fact that I'm being a dickhead. Honestly, I'm surprised he *is* trying and can't really imagine him making an effort with anyone else, but then I think, what the hell is the point?

"Why?" I ask him. "We both know you don't really want

to go. What are we even doing here? You're Chris's brother. We don't even want anyone knowing we hung out today. And then we kiss which was obviously a big-ass mistake. It just…it would make more sense just to go back to the way things have always been between us."

There's a pause and then… "Yeah… Yeah, I guess you're right."

I really didn't want to be right. My stomach twists, gets heavy.

"Thanks for lunch." I get out, and Levi doesn't say a word as I close the door and walk away.

CHAPTER NINE

Levi calls me four times over the next two days and I ignore all of them. It's a weak move on my part. I know it, but I still do it. There just isn't a point in the two of us hanging out. He's going through some shit, and I can sympathize. But if he only wants me around as a sounding board—and he's going to act like the whole world came crashing down because he had his tongue in my mouth—fuck that and fuck him. I'm not going to spend time with a dude who freaks out because he kissed me, when he wouldn't freak out over kissing another guy.

It's early, around seven the day before Christmas Eve. My dad was banging around not long ago, getting ready for work and now, even though I'm willing my eyes to close, they won't. It's too fucking early to be up, but since my brain won't shut down long enough for me to pass out, I push out of bed and take a quick shower.

I'm brushing my teeth when I hear a knock at the door. Dad has to have left by now, so I spit, rinse my mouth and head to my room to find clothes. Who the hell would be coming by before eight o'clock in the morning? They better be telling me I won a shit-ton of money.

Pulling on a T-shirt and a pair of sweats over my boxers, I hear another knock. "I'm coming." They're obviously eager to hand me my check so I don't stop for coffee on my way to meet them.

Without looking through the peephole I pull open the door. Levi stands there with a cup holder filled with two cups and a bag. His hair's hanging in his face and he shakes it out before shrugging, like I'm supposed to be the one to tell him why he's here.

I'd be lying if I didn't admit my pulse goes a little wild at the sight of him. It's as though we're in some parallel universe where Levi Baxter gives a shit about me.

"Hey. I couldn't sleep. Since you ignore my phone calls I decided not to give you a choice and came over here. But look, I brought sugar and caffeine. Points for me, right?" He smiles and damned if it's not contagious. I have to force myself not to return it. But then, that's Levi—he can get what he wants, even from me. There's a small part of me who hates him for that.

Jerking my head toward the house, I surrender to his power and take a step backward. Levi gets the message and comes inside. My house. Levi Baxter is in my house, and I'm stuck between the urge to tell him to leave and to pull him closer.

"I was worried I'd wake you up, but you look like you just got out of the shower."

"My dad woke me up when he was getting ready for work. I couldn't fall back asleep. You always rise with the sun now?" I lead him toward the kitchen. Levi hands me one of the coffees and I take it but don't drink any.

"Yeah, I've had trouble sleeping the past few years."

What the fuck? "Few years? Maybe you should have that checked."

Levi laughs. "It's stress-related. My doctor knows. It's not consistent or anything. It just hits every once in a while. Your phone break, or what?"

For some reason, I didn't expect him to call me out on not responding to his calls. "No."

"So this is what it feels like to get brushed off, huh? Who'd have thought?" When I roll my eyes he continues, "I'm kidding, Toby. I've gotten the brush off plenty. I told you that."

My stomach twists and I set the coffee down, not in the mood for it. Leaning against the table, Levi watches, waiting. He doesn't take his eyes off me, his stare so intense it finds every crack, every little sliver of a place it can seep inside me. I want to ask him what he sees. Want to know what I look like through his eyes. Does he see a half-black, gay kid without a mom? The one who doesn't leave Chris's side because he can't handle getting close to anyone else and risk losing them?

"I thought we settled everything the other day," I say finally.

"And I think that's fucking stupid. Why can't we hang out?"

I don't get why in the hell he suddenly wants to get to know me. "What are you doing, man?" This isn't him. None of it.

"I don't know. Why are you so pissed at me? Yeah you're Chris's friend but what's the big deal if you're my friend, too? I told you the kiss was a mistake. Why can't we just forget about it and move the fuck on?"

It's that last comment that pushes me over the edge. I shove away from the counter, my muscles coiled tight in anger. "Because you've been a dick to us our whole lives! You always thought you were too good for us. You treated Chris like shit and the whole fucking time I still had a hard-on for you. Jesus, I used to jack off to thoughts of you. That's what made me really realize I was gay. The whole time I hid it from Chris because it already pissed him off that everyone thought the sun rose and set on your ass. And then you come back and act like a totally different person. You want to spend time with me, kiss me and then say *oh that was a mistake* because even though you swing both ways, you're obviously still too good for me. You act like I wanted to marry you instead of just bone you, and then you show up at my house with coffee and donuts like—oh fuck."

Levi's body slams into mine. I stumble backward, hitting the wall, Levi squeezes my body between it and him. He smells like soap and coffee. His body's hot and hard, molded against me. He pushes forward, his erection rubbing against mine, the friction making pleasure thrum through me. I don't have time to form a clear thought before we're mouth to mouth the same way we're body to body. His tongue pushes in and I let it. Suck it, before feeding him mine as well.

There's a vibration when he moans; it radiates from Levi into me, making my cock get even harder.

His hands slide up and he grabs the sides of my face. I squeeze his tight ass, and my reward is a second moan from him as he kisses deeper, rubs off on me, so fucking close it's like he wants to climb inside me.

Levi's mouth slides down my neck. He sucks my skin into his mouth.

But then my stupid brain takes over when really I just want to turn the damn thing off and follow my dick's lead. "What the hell are we doing?" I ask.

Levi just shrugs, still kissing at the tender skin of my throat. "You said you wanted me back then. The question now is do you still? Because I'm telling you, Toby, I don't know when it happened, but I want you now."

CHAPTER TEN

I take a few seconds to let his words sink in before my brain listens to my dick and goes quiet. It's sex. We both want it and right now that's all that matters. Any weirdness it could cause is in the future and I'll worry about it later.

"Let's go." I lead Levi to my childhood bedroom, and I'll admit it's kind of strange to see him in my space. The second we're inside, I close the door and drop to my knees. A slight pain shoots through my right knee when it hits the floor. It doesn't matter, though. Nothing fucking matters as I work the button and zipper on Levi's jeans.

"You used to jack off thinking about me?" There's laughter in his voice, but I'm too horny to return it.

"Shut up."

"I never fucking knew. I mean, I'm not sure how I would have felt about it back then anyway, but—"

"Shut up," I say again. If he's talking, he's thinking, and right now all either of us should do is *feel* so our brains can't tell us this is a bad idea.

"Holy shit, this is so fucking weird. Seeing you on your knees. You're Chris's—"

"Can we please not talk about your brother?" And then I reach into his boxer briefs and palm his dick.

"Oh fuck. Yeah, not talking. Put your mouth on me, Toby."

I slide my hands around to his ass, palming it beneath his jeans and underwear before I push them down.

And then I do just as he said, suck him into my mouth, feel the veins with my tongue. All that hardness covered in soft skin that tastes of salt.

He holds onto the back of my head as I work him, as I show him what I can do. Levi breathes hard, moans, moves his hips as I take him as deep as I can get him. Drive him wild the way he's always done to me.

I feel him tense up, know he's getting close, and then he's pulling me to my feet and pushing his tongue into my mouth again.

"Do you have condoms?" he asks between kisses and I wonder why in the hell he doesn't have any.

"Yeah." I grab my wallet from my dresser, pull a condom out and a small package of lube, then toss them both to the bed.

"Jesus, you've gotten sexy." He pushes his hands under my shirt and I pull it off for him. Watch as his pale hand explores my darker chest, hiss when his thumb rubs my copper-colored nipple. This is fucked up and confusing but none of that is going to make me stop it.

"Take the rest of your clothes off," he says.

Reaching out, I stroke him again, just because I can. He's long, slightly curved and full of thick veins that felt good against my tongue.

Levi pulls off his shirt, so I shove down my sweats and underwear. He's watching me, eyes glued to my body, dark and stormy with lust. For just a second, I let myself revel in the thought of turning Levi on that much.

"Look at all that caramel skin." He winks at me, and this time I do laugh. Fucker.

"Stop talking and keep going," I tease.

"Holy shit." Levi strokes himself, steps forward and flicks his tongue over my nipple, sucks it into his warm mouth and then does the same to my left. I'm so hard I feel like I could explode at any second.

We start kissing, eating at each other's mouths like we're starving as we tumble onto the bed. He pulls away when we're lying down, grabs the condom, and opens it before rolling it down my erection. "When I'm with a guy, I want to be pounded. That okay with you?"

I damn near have to hold myself off from blowing my load and ruining this whole thing before getting inside him. My vision swims and my body gets tight like I'm amped up on something. I guess I am—lust. "Stupid fucking question."

Levi goes down on his stomach, ass in the air. I rub my hand over the creamy globes and watch him tremble, watch his back arch in a sexy, come-take-me way. Ripping the package of lube open, I spread some on Levi and then on myself.

He moans, pushing toward me as I rub him, push a finger in, pull it out and then slide it back in again. "Just take me,

Toby."

Well, okay, since he asked so nicely. I line myself up and then slowly stretch him, working my way inside.

"Oh, fuck. Fuck yeah," he mumbles over and over until I'm buried deep. And then I just have to stay still so I don't fucking blow. He's tight, so damned tight. I need to come so badly I ache, and when Levi pushes back, I have to move.

I thrust into him, pull out and then do it over and over. Reaching around, I rub my finger over the head of his erection, stroke his hard length in unison with every slam of my hips. "You feel amazing." A tight, hot cave.

"So do you. Go harder."

He doesn't have to ask twice. I do exactly as he says, railing him the way he seems to need. Before I know it, he's tensing up, releasing, making each tug on his dick glide more smoothly and then he shoots again. I'm right behind him, groaning out my orgasm before crumpling down on the bed with him.

CHAPTER ELEVEN

The room's quiet except the sound of deep breathing. It echoes in my head–*Levi's mine, Levi's mine, Levi's mine.*

His left leg is thrown over me, the hairs rubbing against my thigh. I should say something…but what? I just screwed Levi—as in I honestly had my dick in his ass and didn't just dream it. I'm not sure the reality of it has sunk in yet.

I'd fantasized about having him for years. Lots of those fantasies included visions of how I would feel afterward—the satisfaction of having someone so far out of reach, of proving to myself I could have someone as amazing as Levi Baxter, always came with a certain amount of pride and chest-banging. The reality is different. I don't feel like bragging about a conquest or thumping my chest. Honestly, I can't say exactly what it does feel like, only that it's somehow *more.*

And that ladies and gentlemen, is scary as fuck.

"I needed that." Levi breaks our silence.

I pull the condom off and toss it into the trash. "Yeah, me too."

He pushes out of the bed, and I get this sudden pinch in my chest. I'm not sure why I'm surprised he's leaving. Not sure if I care either, or maybe I just don't want to admit that I do.

I watch his ass move as he walks over to his jeans. Instead of putting them on, he reaches into the front pocket and pulls out a baggie. "Do you mind?" After opening the bag, he holds up a joint and a lighter.

Huh. Levi smokes weed. I don't know why I didn't see that coming. "Nope."

He climbs back into bed with me, lights up and takes a hit before passing it to me. I don't smoke real often, but I'd say this is a good excuse to toke up. Neither of us speaks as we lie naked in my double bed, passing a joint back and forth, the sweet burn deep in my lungs.

When we finish, Levi rolls onto his stomach, folds his arms and lets his head rest on them while looking at me. He has a calmness about him right now, a lazy grin on his thin lips.

"You a pothead now, Doc?" I tease.

His smile dims slightly, making me wish I hadn't brought up the doctor thing. "Nope. Calms me down, though. Turns out not knowing what the fuck you want to do with your life—even when you thought you had the whole thing mapped out—can make you anxious as hell."

A tornado of guilt wreaks havoc on my insides. "I'm sorry."

"Don't be. You didn't know. Plus, you screwed my brains out so you're forgiven."

He reaches over and runs a hand up my chest. It's like his finger is magnetic, and every good feeling in my body is a shard of metal, all drawn to where he touches, following his every movement as he makes invisible shapes on my skin. "What are you going to do?"

He doesn't pull his hand back, still tracing things I can't see. "I'm gonna finish what I started. That's who I am, Toby. I'll love it eventually. I have to."

Shaking my head, I let out a deep breath. "People change. I used to want to be a paleontologist, and now I don't. You used to only bone girls. Just because you used to want something, doesn't mean you always have to. You can't live your life doing something that doesn't make you happy."

Maybe it sounds dramatic but I feel like if Levi Baxter—a guy who's always lived life the way he wanted and enjoyed the hell out of it—feels like he has to go into a profession that might depress him and give him anxiety, what hope do the rest of us have?

"Maybe it will."

"Maybe it won't."

"You're always trying to argue with me. I think you like it." Levi pinches one of my nipples and I swat his hand. He's the one who likes to argue.

"I'm serious, man. What's the big deal? I don't understand why you'd keep going if it's not what you want." I'm not trying to be a dickhead, just trying to make sense of it.

Levi pulls his hand away and I immediately want it back. "Because something is better than nothing. Continuing with my original plan and finishing med school is better than flaking out, right? I don't want to just sit around, not knowing

who I am or what I want. Maybe that makes me a stuck-up
bastard, but I can't be that person, Toby."

I'm not sure what to say to that and Levi doesn't really
give me the chance to think about it. "I'm tired. Is it cool if I
pass out here for a little while?"

"Yeah, no problem."

He scoots closer to me, his skin hot, and wraps an arm
around me before closing his eyes. That easily he goes to
sleep, and I think maybe we can do this—find a way to be
friends who maybe fuck around from time to time, because it
seems like the guy who's always had everything is now alone.

CHAPTER TWELVE

Christmas Eve is like the day that never ends. I hang around the house with my dad who's either sitting silently in front of the TV or working. This is the only house I've ever lived in, and even though sometimes it felt lonely or stifling, I've never hated it. Maybe it's the holiday, or maybe it's all the weird shit that's happened on my vacation so far, but for the first time in my life my own home feels strange. I'm not totally sure why, but I feel it. Feel it in my chest and under my skin—like everything I do is just...off somehow.

When I go to bed, my sheets smell like Levi. I had real experience to draw from when I rubbed one out thinking of him last night. We'd taken a short nap and then he'd headed home. I haven't talked to him since. The Baxters celebrate Christmas on Christmas Eve, so I don't want to interrupt their family time.

On Christmas morning, I roll out of bed around ten. When I make my way to the kitchen, Dad's sitting at the table with a cup of coffee in front of him, steam rising from the top.

"Mornin'." I scratch my head as I pad across the floor to

the pot and fill myself a cup.

"Merry Christmas."

"Merry Christmas to you, too." I look around and notice the ham he's ordered—he orders one every year—is resting on the counter. We'll just have to warm it up, and for Christmas dinner we'll eat that, boxed scalloped potatoes and green beans.

When I sit down across from him, he pushes an envelope toward me. "I figured money is the best gift for you. I'm not sure what kind of stuff you might need when you get back to San Francisco. That way you can buy whatever you want."

"Thanks, Dad." For some reason, my fingers shake as I open the envelope. There's some cash and a generic card inside with six words in my dad's messy handwriting.

I'm proud of you.
Love, Dad

It's the first time in my life he's ever told me he's proud of me. My chest gets tight, my fingers still trembling as I read the card again. Without thinking, I push to my feet, walk over and hug him. "Thank you."

He gives me an awkward pat on the back. "Let me go get my gift for you," I say. It's a stupid-ass sports trivia book. I had no clue what the hell to get him.

"It can wait." Before I reply, my phone rings and Dad says, "Go ahead and get it."

Without looking at the screen, I know who it'll be. "It's

probably just Chris wanting to wish me a Merry Christmas."
I've been a dickhead to Chris for the last few days. He's tried
to get me to come over more than once, wanting me to meet
Gemma, but I haven't made it there yet, mostly because of
conflicting feelings about his brother—weirdness over
spending time with him, then anger at him, and finally
because I had sex with him.

"Merry Christmas!" Chris says right after I pick up the
phone.

"Hey, man. Same to you. What's up?"

"Nothing. What are you guys doing?" He knows the
answer, which he makes obvious when he continues, "Why
don't you come over for a bit? You can eat some leftovers
with us."

For a brief second I consider saying yes. Things are so
much more alive at his house, but it feels wrong to leave.
Especially after the card my dad just gave me.

"You can meet Gem," Chris says. "So far you just look
like an asshole since you haven't come over here yet."

"Ha, ha," I tease as I watch my dad take a drink of his
coffee. "Screw you."

"I'm serious, man. Come hang out with us. She's only
going to be here a few more days."

Guilt spreads through my chest. It's important to Chris
that I meet her. I know it is. He's had my back for most of my
life, and he doesn't ask much of me. Hell, I *want* to meet her.
But then I look at my dad again. He yawns even though he
just got up. I'm not feeling guilt just for being an ass to Chris,
I'm feeling guilt about my dad, for his life, for him acting
tired and old despite how young he is. He wears his loneliness

carved in his skin—the letters might be in the form of wrinkles and weariness, but they are there for the world to see. I have to wonder if part of his loneliness is my fault.

He told me he's proud of me and now it's my turn to take the next step.

"How about tomorrow?" I tell Chris. "I'm going to make dinner with my dad and watch some football." Maybe all it would take to make a difference is if I make a few pushes into his life. He could be waiting for me to make the first move. Maybe he doesn't know how to start the conversation any more than I do.

"What?" Dad looks up from his coffee. "No, you go ahead. Go hang out with Chris. I don't need help tossing a ham into the oven to warm up. We can eat when you get home."

My throat gets tight, itchy, words trapped inside it. It's fucking Christmas. We should spend the day together.

Dad shakes his head. He must be able to tell I'm going to argue with him because he says, "Seriously, Toby. Don't worry about me. This is your vacation. You only have a limited time home to see your friends."

To see my friends. He doesn't care I only have a couple weeks to see him, as well.

"Go on," Dad adds.

"Is that Toby?" I hear Elaine say in the background. "Tell him to come and eat with us! We have enough food."

Dad tells me to go yet again when Mrs. Baxter asks me to come. This very conversation has happened hundreds of times. You'd think I'd be used to how he pushes me away, encouraging me to spend time with a family that isn't really mine.

Yeah, you'd think I'd be used to it, but there's this empty feeling in my chest that says maybe I'm not.

"Get your ass over here, T. Come hang out with us. You gotta give her the bro test, man. You're my boy. I trust your opinion."

And even though I've never talked to Chris about my dad, I know he gets it. I know that's why he's pushing so hard for me to come over right now. He probably knows what it's like here—Dad and I sitting in awkward silence. Eating crappy food and watching a game I couldn't give a shit about. He's always been the kind of friend who wanted to make sure I felt welcomed.

And maybe I shouldn't be, but I'm pissed at my dad for not being the same kind of man.

I think about what it might be like if I go over to the Baxter's house. It'll be awkward, being around Levi and pretending things are the same as they've always been, but there's not a doubt in my mind we can handle it. In a lot of ways, nothing has changed other than the fact that we got off together, and he told me something he hasn't shared with anyone else.

Okay, so maybe a lot has changed.

"Yeah…yeah, I'll be right there."

CHAPTER THIRTEEN

When I get to Chris's, there's Christmas music coming from inside the house. It's almost enough to make me want to turn around and walk away, but I don't. Jesus, I've been a grumpy bastard lately.

After a quick knock, I hear Chris yell, "Come in!" so I push the door open. He's sitting on the couch with a girl next to him. She's Native American and Japanese. I only know this from Chris telling me. She has long, black hair that goes almost down to her ass. She's thin, and from the looks of it, a little on the short side. She's gorgeous. If I'm being honest, I can see why he was nervous for his brother to meet her. Gemma looks like a girl who would catch Levi's eye.

Chris turns my way. "Hey, man. What's up?"

Gemma pushes off the couch and gives me a smile that, if I were straight, would probably make me fall in love with her, too. "Finally!" she says. "If it isn't the famous Toby. I was beginning to think you didn't exist." She walks my way and I hold out my hand, but Gemma ignores it and hugs me. I stiffen up slightly. Being touchy-feely with people I don't know is not one of my favorite things.

"I could say the same thing about you. A woman who likes this guy? I had to see you to believe it." When she lets go of me, I take a step backward.

"He's alright." She winks at Chris and he rolls his eyes before wrapping his arm around her. "He's more than alright," Gemma adds. The look Chris gives her says that where this girl is concerned, he's even more gone than I thought.

"Where is everyone?" I ask as Gemma rejoins Chris on the couch. What I really mean is where is Levi?

"Dad's on call at the hospital and he got called in. Mom ran to drop off some food donations at the shelter. Levi took off this morning, back to California."

My body tenses up. My chest gets a heavy feel to it. What. The. Fuck. He left? He went back to school on Christmas? Didn't even say anything to me despite what happened the other day? It's not as though I thought we were a couple or anything. But hell, I at least deserve a "Thanks for the fuck, I'm heading out of town" call, don't I?

"Can you believe that shit?" Chris asks, shaking his head. "What an asshole. I guess he had the opportunity to have a talk with some important surgeon about shit that shouldn't fucking matter on Christmas, so he bailed. Selfish bastard."

I plop down on the other couch, still running over what he said in my mind to make sure I heard him correctly.

I can't believe he left and didn't say a word to me. And what a lame excuse. There is no doctor. I know it and Levi knows it, even though the rest of them don't.

"Has Chris always been like this about his brother?" Gemma asks me.

I try to focus on her and stop tripping out over something I shouldn't care about. Levi and I had sex. He left. End of story. "Yep."

"You can't say he's not a spoiled asshole, T. You know he is."

It takes me a minute to figure out how to reply to Chris. Yeah, Levi can be a dickhead. He always *was* a dickhead. But the guy I hung out with recently—the man lying in bed with me the day before yesterday—was different.

"People change," Gemma answers Chris for me. "He gave you a sweet card with your Christmas gift. It was really nice. Your relationship can't be all bad."

"Oh yeah…like one time he's nice and that's supposed to make up for all the times he was an ass? I can't think of a time he wasn't a jerk to me." Chris shakes his head and I can tell he's truly annoyed. "Like the time he got us kicked out of a party I'd been looking forward to all year. Or all the times they gave me shit on the football team because I was Levi Baxter's brother, but yet where he was the king of the field, I sucked. And who could forget when he stole my high school girlfriend?"

There's this strange tug inside me, this pull that tells me to stick up for Levi. It's another layer of complication between me and the two Baxter boys that I don't know how to deal with. They're brothers. They're both competitive guys. Of course they're going to fight about shit. But Chris is my best friend and it's not my place to defend Levi. Especially when everything Chris said is true. Not that he and Bridget were really together, but they were something. I sigh and try to say something comforting to Chris. "Yeah, I—"

"Here, Toby," Gemma interrupts. "Levi asked me to give you this when he left." She pulls an envelope from her purse and I practically feel the blast of heat from Chris. I can guarantee he's wondering why Levi would be giving me something.

After taking the envelope from her, I try to put it into my pocket, but Chris asks, "What is it?"

Fuck. I shrug. "I don't know. I'm sure he's just trying to be a nice guy." But Chris won't let it go and I know it, so I open the envelope and see tickets inside and a short note.

Toby,

Hope you enjoy the show. If you ask, Chris will go with you. For some reason, I have a feeling you won't ask, though. And... I'm sorry...fuck, for everything, I guess. Thanks for everything, too.

Levi

There's an empty feeling in my chest I'm not sure was there before. If it was, I didn't know it, but now it's taking over, spreading through me. I'm pissed and confused and...hell, mostly sad, I think. Sad because my dad can't even fucking talk to me and sad because Levi is doing something he hates. Sad because I feel like I was really getting to know him for the first time and now he's gone. Sad that he left without saying goodbye the same way my mom did...

"What is it?" Chris asks again, and I know I have to

answer him.

"Tickets to see Jekyll and Hyde. I said something about wanting to go when your mom had the party for us. He must have heard me." And now I'm lying to Chris, something I've never had to do before. It's a virus eating away at my gut.

I don't stay long at Chris's. I'm pretty sure he can tell something's up but he doesn't ask. Not long after his mom gets home, I make up an excuse about getting back home to cook with my dad.

He's asleep on the chair when I get there. I bring his Christmas gift down and set it next to him, then lie on the couch and watch the game I don't care about, thinking of Levi who bailed on me and my dad who can't find it in himself to care about much of anything.

He wakes up not long after. He says he likes the gift, but I can't tell if he really does. We cook and finish watching the game. We probably do other shit, too. But it's stuff that doesn't matter, stuff I won't remember.

We continue the rest of my break that way, minus the cooking together. He works, I chill, we share a few words and that's about it. Levi was right and I don't ask Chris to go with me to the play. Chris and I hang out a few times, but I'm being a sullen bastard and make up excuses to avoid him.

Levi and I don't talk again, but I guess I should have expected that. His head's all screwed up, we boned, that's the end of it.

Still, I don't delete his number from my phone.

CHAPTER FOURTEEN

February

San Francisco

"Toby! Hey, wait up," Cherise, a girl from a few of my classes, calls from behind me.

Her boyfriend Brian chimes in right behind her, "If you wait, you're fucked!"

I can't help but smile as I turn around. I should have known I wouldn't make it off campus without her catching up with me. She's pushy. Cool, but pushy. She's got it in her mind that we need to be friends. Not in the annoying-ass way some people do, trying to collect gay boys like we're pets, but still she's a little heavy-handed for my taste.

"It's your birthday, right?" she asks when they catch up to me.

Brian mumbles, "I told you," before I ask, "Did I tell you that?" They fall into step with me as I go. "Because I don't

95

think I would have told you that."

"You mentioned it offhandedly. Something about not having to use your fake ID anymore."

Shit. I need to be more careful. "Yeah, it's my birthday." Since I need to catch the bus to get home (it's less expensive than driving around here), I don't slow down, the three of us walking through the damp, foggy day.

"So you're twenty-one now."

Smiling at her, I reply. "I'm aware. Nothing gets by you."

Cherise rolls her eyes and Brian laughs. "She's hinting, man. She wants to go out for your birthday."

"Or if you don't want to go out, there's a party. Since you're actually legal, I figured you'd want to hit up a bar or club or something."

And she obviously just assumes I would go by myself. Honestly, I probably would, but her assumption makes me frown. "I considered it. My roommate Xavier and I might go do something." Ha. See? I have people I can ask to hang out. There's more than just Xavier, if I want company. Her lips purse slightly and I can tell she didn't expect my answer. "What the hell?" I ask. "You thought I didn't have anyone to go out with?"

We hit the street and I stop to wait for the bus. The city's moving like crazy around us, cars driving, people walking. It's so alive. That's my favorite thing about living in a big city, the pulsing energy and the thriving diversity everywhere you look.

"No, no. I know you have people you hang out with

sometimes. You're just…funny about certain things, about letting people close. So I thought your birthday would be a secret. You have to admit you're shady like that, and you've been particularly growly since you came back from break last month."

After hefting my bag up my shoulder, I cross my arms. "I'm not growly." Am I? I've never seen myself that way. Yeah, I don't like to share my business with the world but that's different than being an asshole, which is basically what she's saying.

"You've been kind of growly the past month, dude," Brian throws in but I can tell he's just trying to give me shit. Or stick up for his girl so he gets laid tonight.

"Do you guys have a point? I'd like to wait for my bus in peace." Oh yeah, I'm growly.

"I just thought maybe we could all go do something. Your roommate can come too, if he wants. Brian and I wanted to go out, but we're not sure about hitting up a party. I figured your birthday would be a good excuse to go out. I've only seen you at one party since we got back to school."

What the hell? That can't be true. I go out all the time.

"You've seemed a little down," she adds.

Which should definitely not be the case. There's nothing for me to be down about. In fact, I should still be feeling stoked that I got a piece of Levi Baxter's ass. "School's kicking my butt. And yeah, I'll probably go out tonight."

"He probably wants to go get laid tonight, Cherise. Not hang out with us."

Brian is right. Not that I have a problem with them, but

hell, it is my birthday.

"Well, it's not like he has to hang out with us all night!" She rolls her eyes and a strand of blond hair falls in her face. Brian pushes it behind her ear for her. The movement seems like such a natural reflex for him and for some reason, it makes me wonder if my dad used to do things like that for my mom, or if she ever did for him. I don't remember stuff like that. I sure as hell know I've never done something similar to anyone. It's so simple yet intimate at the same time.

"Brian's right." I pull myself out of my useless thoughts. "And yeah, I wouldn't mind chilling but I'll probably go to a gay club."

They both laugh and then Brian shrugs before putting an arm around Cherise. "I don't give a shit about that. Gay club, straight club, they all serve alcohol, so it's the same to me. I'm secure enough in my manhood that it doesn't matter. I have my girl so I'm not looking for anyone else, anyway."

I hadn't really expected him to say that, but I'm still not sure I want to include them in my plans for the night. I'm twenty-one, horny, and want to get drunk, so why does it matter if they go?

"Come on, Toby. Let us treat you to a drink. We can talk about that paper for English Literature. I trust your judgment and I'm really curious how you feel about—"

"No!" both Brian and I say at the same time.

"What?" Her eyes go wide, but I can tell she knows what we mean.

"We're not going out and talking about school, baby. That's why it's the weekend. We're going out to get faded."

Cherise's cheeks turn pink. "Toby's really smart. I just wanted to get his opinion on—"

"Shh." He puts a finger to her lips. "We said no. You're breaking the rule of weekends. No school shit. Give Toby your phone so he can put his number in."

Cherise pouts but does as he says. I'm fine with exchanging numbers, but my plans are still up in the air as far as I'm concerned. I know my roommate Xavier will be looking for the same kind of action I'll be seeking tonight, so my first choice for company will likely be him. We're cool, but we don't usually hang out much.

I look up to see the bus nearly hitting the curb as it rumbles to a stop in front of me. "I'll let you guys know if I'm going out."

They both wave and I get on the bus to head back to my apartment. The second I fall into the seat, my phone rings. What the fuck? I have no idea why I'm so popular today. Pulling it out of my pocket, I see Chris's name on the screen. "I'm officially twenty-one and will be partying without you," I say instead of hello. He laughs.

"That's because you had to go to school in San Francisco."

"No, it's your fault because you had to go back East."

"Happy birthday, man. What are you going to do?"

I don't know I'm completely sure of the details until I open my mouth and say, "There's this club in town...Blue Velvet. I've heard it's pretty dope. I think I'm going to go there."

Yeah, it's decided. I'm going to go out. I'm going to

invite Xavier and text Cherise and Brian. I'm tired of sitting around and moping because some dude I slept with bailed and hasn't talked to me in weeks.

My childhood fantasy came true. I had Levi Baxter, and now it's time to move the fuck on.

CHAPTER FIFTEEN

I answered Xavier's ad for a roommate, and that's how the whole living-together thing started. My sophomore year I wanted off campus. The price for living on campus is more expensive and even with my loans, I struggle for money. Although I preferred living on my own, rooming with someone was the only way to make getting out of the dorms an option. He's cool. A little different, but cool. He spends most of his home time playing video games. When he's gone, I have no idea where he is or what he does. We get along alright, and stay out of each other's way. Neither of us gives a shit about the other one bringing a guy home, so it works.

We don't really hang out that often, but I know Xavier likes to hit up clubs, so I'm sure he'll be down to go tonight. We've gone like twice together.

When I get back to our apartment, he's on the couch with a cigarette in his mouth and a video game controller in his tattooed hands, his black-painted fingernails moving swiftly across the buttons. If he's gotten ready for the day, he'll be wearing eyeliner as well. His skin's maybe a shade lighter than mine. His last name is Ramos, so I know his dad is

Hispanic. Not sure about his mom, though.

"What are you doing tonight?" The door closes with a soft click behind me.

"Chillin'. You?" He doesn't turn away from the game.

After tossing my backpack to the table, I watch the video screen for a few moments. Xavier pushes his dark hair out of his eyes but still doesn't stop the action on the screen.

"I'm twenty-one today." I shrug. "I thought maybe we could go out."

When he finally turns my way, Xavier's brows pull together. "That's the first time you've asked me to hang out with you."

I'm not sure why this matters. "We've gone out."

"But you've never asked. No biggie. I just thought it was funny. I think you want to be my friend. I wasn't sure at first. You're weird with people."

Weird with people? Who just throws that out there at someone? "Are you high?"

Xavier laughs. "Yeah, that doesn't change anything. It's just funny. When we met up to see about you moving in here, I wasn't sure it would work. You're a little too pretty-boy. I thought we'd bump heads, but then I realized you're cool. A little distant, but cool. Yeah, I'm down to go out tonight, though. Where we going?"

My mind stutters as I try to keep up with all his subject changes. The guy has no filter, and he doesn't know me. But what he said about me being distant and weird with people bugs me. I'm *not* distant with people. No, I don't want to be close with everyone I meet, but there's nothing wrong with that. Most people let you down. The less people I allow that opportunity, the better. Chris is the only one who's never let me down.

He leans forward, stubs out his cigarette in the ashtray, and then walks over to dump it in the trash on the balcony. He doesn't smoke inside very often and when he does, he always dumps the ashtray right after.

Trying to push his words out of my head, I say, "I figured we could check out Blue Velvet."

"Sounds dope." The slider sticks slightly, but then he pulls it closed. "I'm gonna take a nap so I'm ready for tonight. I had to be up way too fucking early this morning." He walks out of the living room, down the hall and into his room. He closes the door without another word. For some reason I'm stuck in the same spot, thinking about everything he said.

***

"You look good." Xavier laughs as we walk down the street toward Blue Velvet. It's only about a twenty-minute walk from our apartment, which could possibly feel like an eternity when I'm walking home tonight, *if* I come home tonight, but it's a chance I'm willing to take.

I'm wearing red Converse, black jeans and a tight, red shirt. I like the way red looks against my skin. "But still pretty-boy?" I tease him about what he said earlier.

"Yeah, but that's okay. I'm an equal-opportunity lover. I don't do roommates though, so we're screwed. Sorry to break your heart."

A laugh jumps out of my mouth. He's a cool guy. It makes me wonder why I don't hang out with him more often. "Excuse me while I cry. Now I'm going to have to drown my sorrows in my beer tonight."

Xavier chuckles and we finish our walk to the club. Brian and Cherise are waiting in front of the old building with the blue awning. She notices me right away and smiles.

"That your people?" Xavier asks. It's my reflex to say no, but then I remember what he said earlier about me being distant, so I pretend I'm closer to them than I am.

"Yeah."

I make introductions and then the four of us wait in line to get into the club. It doesn't take very long despite the long line, and this time, I get to use my real ID instead of my fake one.

The bouncer, a tall black guy with dreads, winks at me and tells me happy birthday as we go inside.

"Let's hit the bar. I'll buy you a drink for your birthday." Xavier heads toward the alcohol. Hip-hop blasts through the speakers as hundreds of people dance and move together. There's a roped off section with a few tables, people in every chair. The club is full of a wide variety of people—young and old, male and female, suits, and jeans.

"Brian and I have your second one. It's your birthday. You shouldn't have to buy your own drinks," Cherise chimes in.

"No, you don't—"

"Toby!" She yells over the loud music that vibrates in my chest, and I roll my eyes at her.

Dude. What's wrong with not wanting everyone to buy my shit? "Yeah, sure. Whatever. Buy me drinks. That works for me."

Xavier and Cherise both buy me shots when we get to the bar. The first burns more than the second as I let the warm fireball slide down my throat, one drink after the other.

"Do you wanna dance?" Xavier steps in close to me, a hand at my waist. I can tell he repainted his nails. He's wearing his black eyeliner that matches his hair and a black button-down shirt, left open with a white tee under it. I agree with him on the no roommate thing, but if we didn't live together, I'd definitely hit on him. That doesn't mean we can't dance though.

"Yeah. Let's do it." The four of us make our way to the dance floor. Every so often I catch a glimpse of half-naked men dancing on tables and playing the crowd to get money shoved in their underwear. But mostly I just concentrate on dancing. I'm sweating and Cherise is laughing, and true to his word, Brian looks as comfortable as every other guy in this place. Not that he shouldn't be, but some people act screwed up about things like that.

Xavier dances with me, then turns to dance with someone else. When I see Cherise's eyes go wide, I look over my shoulder to see him making out with whoever his new partner is.

"My sheltered little girl." Brian wraps his arms around her as they keep moving. They've been together a long time. I can see it in the way their bodies touch and the familiarity in everything they do.

My heart's beating faster than the music and I have cottonmouth, so I lean forward and say, "I'm going to cruise around, check things out and get a drink."

"We'll come with you!" Cherise yells back. She doesn't

have to yell, though, because the crowds have pushed her so close. In fact, it's getting more crowded in here by the second, hard to breathe and definitely hard to walk. Bodies are packed in around me like a herd of cattle.

Fuck. I'd hoped that wouldn't be her reply. Brian laughs before telling her, "I'm pretty sure he wants to be alone for a while. Or at least not with us. If we see you around later, cool. If not, it was good hanging out with you, man."

Some of the weight eases off my chest. I'm glad he gets it. Plus, in all honesty, they can't really want to spend the night at a gay club with some guy they hardly know. Yeah, I have a few classes with Cherise and we talk in class, but before today, that was the extent of our interaction.

My muscles tense up slightly when she gives me a hug, invading my space. Why do people insist on hugging goodbye and hello when we'll see each other again soon? I've never gotten that. Or why they'd hug someone when they don't even know if that person likes to be touched.

Awkwardly, I pat her on the back, thank her for hanging out with me and then make my escape. This whole day has been odd. I'm ready for some normalcy and hoping like hell I find it, and maybe someone to temporarily enjoy it with, too.

CHAPTER SIXTEEN

The bar's my first stop. I order a shot of Fireball and swallow it in one gulp. The glass hits a little too hard on the bar when I set it down. Everyone's having a good time tonight. I'm twenty-one, horny, and out. What more is there to want?

Nothing. Which is why I can't understand why there's a sour feeling rolling in my gut that has nothing to do with the alcohol. I feel off tonight and I don't know why.

The guy next to me leans closer, his mouth against my ear. "You're entirely too angry for hanging in a place like this."

He's probably exactly what I need. Distraction, fun. "Who says I'm angry?" I lean back and look at him. He's hot. He has dark hair that's buzzed short except for at the top. It's a couple inches long there and styled upward. He's got a pierced ear, a ring in his nose and eyes so blue I'm not sure they're real, lined with black eyeliner. He grins. Oh yeah, he knows I'm looking.

"Maybe I don't need you to say it. Maybe I'm psychic."

He loses a few points with that one, but I decide to keep playing the game with him. It's not like I have anything else going on at the moment. "If you're psychic, what am I thinking?" I cross my arms and wait for him to answer.

"You're considering walking away after my cheesy-ass line, but you think I'm hot so you'll stick around." He winks and if I'm being honest, a low burn starts deep in my gut at his reply.

"That so? What if you're not my type?"

He rolls his eyes as if I'm being ridiculous, and in a lot of ways, I guess I am. "I'm your type. At least for a night. You're mine, too. But I'll make you a deal. I'll buy you another drink, we'll talk and you can decide if I'm right about you. Sound good...?" He draws the last part out like he's fishing for my name, and I figure what the hell and answer him.

"Tobias."

"Nice to meet you, Tobias. I'm Seth." He reaches for my hand and I shake his. "What do you want?"

"Rum and Coke."

"See? I knew you liked me. You could have ordered another shot so you wouldn't have to talk to me for as long."

Oh, he's fucking good. But still. "Or I ordered something that would take me longer to drink because I don't want to leave here with you."

Seth pretends to clutch his chest. "All I've done is be nice to you and you have to go and hurt my feelings that way."

We both laugh and I think again that Seth might be

exactly what I need for my birthday. Not to hang out with people who obviously thought I'd be alone tonight, or someone who thinks I'm distant. And yeah, maybe I need to change the fact that Levi fucking Baxter was the last person I've been with.

Seth winks at me when I don't respond to his previous statement. "I'll win you over, because I have no problem admitting you're sexy as fuck, and I'd leave here with you in a second."

The burn in my gut turns to an ache and heads south, landing in my dick. "I'd reply to that but you already know the answer since you're psychic."

The bartender makes his way to us again. Seth orders us each a rum and Coke, but I pull out the cash to pay for my own. His brows knit together and I can tell he doesn't like it, but he doesn't argue with me about it.

We nurse our drinks and bullshit for the next few minutes. He's from San Francisco, has lived here his whole life. He broke up with his boyfriend a couple months ago and is just looking to have a good time.

He's a cool guy. Would make a good hook-up, which I knew from the start. He's attracted to me and I'm attracted to him. We're both single and those are really the only things to consider.

When I empty my glass, Seth leans closer to me again, "You're gonna say yes. Am I right?" He touches my leg.

I open my mouth to reply, but before I can speak, I hear, "Toby." The voice is soft, but somehow makes its way through the lively sounds of music and people.

Seth's hand slides off my thigh and I turn around to see

Levi standing there, hands stuffed into the pockets of his jeans. Levi, in a club in San Francisco, on my fucking birthday. The same Levi I haven't spoken to since we were in my bed talking and screwing.

"Fuck," Seth says, taking the word right out of my mouth. "My forecast just changed."

I'm close to laughing, but then my muscles tighten up in annoyance. There's no reason for anything to change. Levi and I have already handled our business.

I turn to Seth and say, "No, it's cool. This is just my friend's brother, Levi. Levi, this is Seth." He's always emphasized that I'm Chris's friend, but he's never proven himself as *my* friend. Still, it almost looks like Levi flinches when I deliberately leave him out of the friend equation.

I watch his face, wondering which Levi has shown up here tonight. The Levi with the cocky mask? Vulnerable, confused Levi? Dickhead Levi from my childhood? Don't know if it's the lighting or the alcohol or just him, but as I stare at his face I'm not sure who this person is, or hell, who the real Levi is. Or even if I care.

Seth chuckles, but I can tell by the tone of his laughter that there's nothing funny to him about this situation. "I'm psychic, remember? Maybe another time, champ. You know where to find me." And then he slides off the stool and walks away.

I pause two beats before sliding off my own stool, pushing my way through the crowd. Fuck Levi for coming here and fuck Seth for walking away like it mattered.

"Toby! Wait up." There's a slight tug on my shirt and I know it's Levi. I pull out of his grasp. Maybe it should mean something that he's following me, but all I can think about is how he just left Coburn without a word. Someone I've known for eleven years and had my dick inside, and then he just bows the fuck out.

"Hey. What the fuck, man? Slow down." He grabs my arm as soon as I get to the other side of the bar.

"A shot of whiskey," I tell the bartender before tossing down some cash. "Why?" I ask Levi. "What's the point? We're not friends, Levi. We never have been. I'm Chris's friend and you and I had sex. That's it." *And then you just fucking left.* I jerk my arm and he lets go. "I'm tired and horny and you just fucked with my hook-up."

"I didn't mean to cock-block you, but maybe you should blame him because there's no way I would have walked away from a guy I wanted just because someone approached and said his name."

Yeah…he has me there. But then, who wants all that drama when it comes to meeting someone at a club? "Maybe so, but that doesn't change anything else."

The bartender hands me my shot, and I drain it. It goes straight to my head, making the room spin slightly. I probably shouldn't have had another drink. After the shots earlier, and then the drink with Seth, my lightweight status is showing.

There's no reason for me to act like this. While my head spins, I wonder why I can't seem to change the way I behave where Levi is concerned. And I guess it took getting drunker than shit to realize I'm pissed at Levi for more reasons than I want to consider. "I'm outta here."

There isn't a doubt in my mind that he's right behind me. I stumble out onto the sidewalk, my stomach twisting and turning, my eyes sensitive like I'm looking straight into a light.

I start to walk and after a few moments he asks from beside me, "Did you go to the play?" His voice is so soft, I hardly hear him. He still sounds all husky and sexy, though.

"No." I close my eyes briefly, but then open them so I don't trip. My feet seem to be moving without any guidance from my brain. A good thing, because my brain has been completely taken over by Levi. It doesn't make sense, how he affects me like this. Doesn't make sense that I give a shit he left or showed up now. I wanted, I had. I desired, I conquered. The end.

"Why not?"

As soon as he asks the question, the answer becomes clear in a way I hadn't seen before. Really fucking clear. Like a big lighthouse shining a high-power beam in my eyes. It's painful. I'd wanted Levi to go to the play with me. Like really fucking wanted him to go. Levi, not anyone else.

"Because I didn't want the tickets. What was that? A pay off for a good lay?" I keep walking and Levi keeps following.

"Fuck you, Toby. You know that's not how it was."

"I do?" Something comes over me and I shove him. Levi stumbles backward a few steps but catches himself.

"Lovers quarrel," a dude says as he walks by laughing, but I ignore him.

Backing up, I lean against a brick wall and realize it's my apartment building. I'd been wrong earlier when I thought the walk would take longer while drunk, because I have no idea how I got here so quickly. And as angry as I am, as fast as my heart is slamming…there's a calmness brewing inside me as well. *It feels good to see someone I actually know. It feels good to see Levi.*

"Did you think I was going to fucking cling to you or something? That I thought sleeping together meant more than it did? It was a hook-up, Levi. I knew that. You could have fucking said something before you left."

There's no pause in his reply, he just puts it out there as though giving me these words are the easiest thing in the world. "I know. I was being an idiot…weak."

What I don't understand is why. What was he afraid of?

"You're drunk," he says. "You have this sort of half-smile, half-frown on your face. I bet you don't realize it. Your eyes are glossy, too. I've never seen you drunk before. It's cute."

I close my eyes as though that will make him unsee me. I don't want him to say shit like that to me. It makes my brain go haywire, trying to make sense of things I need to leave alone. "What are you doing here, man?" Sliding down the wall, I let it hold me up, my knees bent and my head in my hands.

Everything stops spinning when I have my eyes closed.

"I don't know," he says softly, and then, "You know what? Fuck that. I wanted to wish you a happy birthday. I wanted to see you. Maybe it doesn't make sense because it's not like we spent a lot of time together, but hell…I think I missed you, Toby."

It's so crazy to hear something like that come out of his mouth. Five years ago, I would have given my left nut for it. Hell, six months ago I would have, even if it was just because

Levi had been a fantasy of mine for so long.

In some ways, the feeling is still there, this ember of excitement that I've tried to bury the past couple months, but looking at him makes it grow brighter, stronger. Because he's still Levi Baxter and I'm still that kid who used to admire him. Because I see something different in him now than just the good-looking guy I want to bone. Because part of me missed him, too.

And I have no idea how to feel about that. It scares the hell out of me.

That and the knowledge of how much I'd cared when he'd bailed on me.

My stomach seizes, contracts. The sour feeling in my gut shoots upward, and I turn around just in time to empty my stomach all over the sidewalk.

CHAPTER SEVENTEEN

This moment is a flashback to my childhood where I'd do stupid, embarrassing shit all the time—trip and fall in the middle of class, dump my lunch tray in the cafeteria, immediately forget the answer to every question as soon as a teacher called on me.

I can't believe I just vomited on the sidewalk like I'm fourteen and drunk for the first time.

"Hey, you okay?" Levi asks me after nothing comes up when I dry heave.

"I puked."

"You did?" There's laughter in his voice, and as much as I don't want to laugh at him right now, a smile tugs at my lips. No matter what it is, Levi always gets what he wants and this moment is no different.

"You're a prick."

"I know, but I'm a sexy one. Come on, I want to help you get home." He takes a step toward me, but I hold my hand out to stop him. That's the last thing I want. There's no reason

I can't make it up the stairs alone.

"I'm fine. I can handle it. In fact, I already am home. This is my building." As soon as I make it to my feet, my brain throbs, and the world spins. I lean against the building to try and regain my equilibrium.

"Why are you like that with me? You don't want me to help you with anything. Last time we ended up at a club together, you helped me to my room, and that wasn't a big deal."

It's easier not to die if I don't open my eyes, so I keep them closed while talking to him. "It's not just *you* I'm like that with. I like to take care of myself. What's wrong with that?" Judging by what Xavier and Cherise both said to me today, I'm an equal opportunity standoffish guy.

"Yeah, I get that. It's always been how you are, but this is different. You're drunk and I'm helping you get home. If Chris was standing here, you'd let him." His brother's name holds a slight edge when he speaks it.

"Jealous?" I ask even though I know there's not a chance he is. That word isn't in Levi's vocabulary when it comes to self-reflection.

"Maybe."

My eyes jerk open at that, and probably pop the hell out of my head. But dude, Levi would have no reason to be jealous over his brother when it comes to me. He's known me half of my life and never given a shit before.

"Can we not do this right now?" I push off the wall, my brain beating against my skull the whole time.

"Oh, how the tables have turned. I seem to remember

116

you trying to talk to me when I had been drinking."

"Funny guy."

"I'm helping you." He wraps an arm around me, and this time I let him, savor the feel of Levi's strong hold balancing me. He feels so damn good. All of this would be a whole hell of a lot easier if he didn't.

We step inside the building—the entryway is tired and grungy-looking, showing the building's condition and age— which seems to fit my own state right about now. My hand knots in Levi's shirt as he works to keep me upright. He's right. I don't like him seeing me this way. If it were Chris helping me, I wouldn't give a shit. He's my boy and that's all, but things are different with Levi. Things have always been different with Levi. "Elevator's broken. Has been for months."

"Okay." He still lends me his strength as we head to the stairs and begin climbing them.

"It's an old building. The apartment isn't all that. I don't even want to think about how it probably compares to where you're staying."

"I don't give a shit about that." His grip on me tightens, and I like the feel of his fingers pressing into my skin, of his warmth under my hand. *No, no, no. Don't do this, Toby. Don't read shit into this situation that isn't really here.*

It's probably an asshole move, but I remind him, "You would have cared a few years ago."

"So? There doesn't seem to be much about me that's the same as it used to be."

Yeah… Yeah, I'm seeing that.

"At least I know how you have those ripped thigh muscles now. You hike up these things how many times a day?"

"Pfft." I stumble and Levi pulls me closer. I smell the soap on his skin. It smells good, expensive, but I want it gone. I only want to inhale the scent of Levi, his skin and his sweat and nothing else. "I'm not known for being the muscular guy." Getting my mind off the way he smells feels like a good idea right about now.

"Eh. Big isn't all that. What matters is how you're cut. I watched your muscles flex as you slammed into me. I know what I'm talking about."

My heart drops and my foot hits the lip on the stairs. This time I do go down; Levi doesn't get the chance to keep me stable. My knee slams into the wood, but it doesn't matter. The only thing that does is what he just said and how it makes my pulse speed up in excitement. "Don't say things like that to me."

"Why?"

"Because I said not to. Jesus, man. What the hell are we doing?" Ignoring my rattled brain, I push to my feet, do my best to keep myself upright and finish taking the stairs, with Levi on my heels.

"What do you mean, what are we doing? And why do you keep freaking out on me?"

My hand shakes as I unlock the door. Yeah, I could totally close it on him, but I don't. That should tell me something right there, but I pretend it doesn't matter. Levi shuts the door behind me, and then follows me as I head directly to the bathroom. Arms crossed, he leans against the doorjamb watching me brush my teeth. It feels intimate to have him standing there and I end up brushing longer than I need to.

"Hey." Levi's hand wraps around my biceps when I try to make my way out of the bathroom. "I shouldn't have taken off without a word. That's something you do with a guy you pick up in a club, not someone you know. I'm sorry." His eyes look somehow darker, smaller, so fucking troubled. I wonder if that's how I looked after my mom left. Alone. "I just..." He lets his sentence trail off, and as much as my mind is telling me to shut up and just stop doing whatever this is we're doing, I speak.

"Come to my room."

"Just to talk," he says. "I want to talk to you, Toby."

I nod and lead the way, hitting the light when we go inside. My head still feels like a racetrack someone's doing laps around. And I'm suddenly hot, so I pull my shirt off, kick out of my shoes and jeans and fall onto the bed. Maybe I'll just pass out. Maybe I'll wake up and he'll be gone and I won't have to find the words to figure out what's going on inside me.

Things are a whole lot easier in darkness so I close my eyes. There's noise in the room, the door closing and what sounds like Levi sitting on the only chair.

"Fuck," Levi says after a moment of silence. "Your mom left. I know how much that messed you up. I know you probably hate it when shit happens that reminds you of it. I didn't think about it when I bailed. I freaked and I don't know why."

Yes, she left. I don't want to get close to people and lose

119

them. The volley's on my tongue, but doesn't make its way
out of my mouth. Still, my head nods, up and down,
confirming what he said. I don't like to be left. It's easier to
keep my distance than risk that.

"But it shouldn't matter," I tell him. "We slept together,
that's it. Maybe I should just let things go, but now you're
here and I'm trying to make sense of why you are. Why you
came to my house back home, how we ended up in my bed,
and everything else that's gone down."

He doesn't answer right away, the silence stretching on
so long I feel like I'm lost in it, blind and touching the walls
in a dark maze to try to find my way out of it. The walls start
closing in on me, it's getting tighter and darker until I make
myself open my eyes just so I know I'm still in my room,
lying on my bed.

"I'm not going to pretend I get it," he says into the
darkness. "All I know is I felt this sort of peace in my chest
when I saw you during break. My head's all fucked up,
running wild with questions all the damn time—wondering
what I'm going to do, why I feel so lost. Wondering who I
am, and what I want, and being pissed at myself for not
knowing the answers. I felt calm with you… I felt like me for
the first time in too long, even though I don't really know who
that is. Which I'm aware makes no fucking sense, but there
you have it." He huffs, and leans back in the chair. His dark
brown hair hangs over his forehead and his tongue touches his
slender lips. He's working his narrow jaw and all I can think
is that he really is fucking beautiful.

Somehow I know he's not finished so I wait. Wait and
watch him rake a hand through his hair. Watch the strands fall
back in his face. Watch him tap the arm of the chair with a

finger. See his throat move as he swallows.

"I want to hold onto that. I have fun with you, kid." When I roll my eyes, Levi chuckles. "I'm giving you shit, but yeah, why can't we just hang out? Be friends, be fuck buddies. Whatever. Let's just chill. I've known you over ten years. Why is it such a big deal to want to spend time with you?"

This time it's Levi's turn to wait as I sort through the cluster of thoughts in my head, trying to separate them out into things I want to tackle and things I want to ignore. The pieces are coming together now, making a slow burn of excitement start under my skin, while at the same time making me want to tell Levi to fuck off and go away.

He wants to hang out with me because he knows I'm the kid who had a hard-on for him growing up. He's confused and feels weak because he doesn't know what he wants. Being with me makes him feel like that guy again, the cocky bastard with all the answers, who has his perfect life laid out for him. I'm a way for Levi to stay tethered to the past because things were a whole lot easier for him there. He wants to use me, whether he realizes it or not.

If I'm being honest, I can't be pissed at him for it. Because I want to say yes. We'll both be using each other— him to feel like the guy who knows it all, and me because he's my wet dream come true.

I answer by saying, "Chris can't know."

A vein protrudes in his neck, pulsing strong enough that I can see it across the small room. "My brother can't know I'm friends with you? Why not?"

Guilt singes my conscience. He really doesn't know how

his brother feels about him—how deep Chris's resentment or jealousy or whatever the heck it is that drives his feelings toward Levi actually goes. Part of me wants to tell him, but my loyalty to Chris overpowers it. "I don't want to have to explain it. I didn't think you'd care if we keep things on the down low, since your family doesn't know you're bi, anyway."

"I didn't plan to tell him I slept with you, but I'm also not ashamed of being with you. I have zero problems with people knowing I'm attracted to men. I'm not ashamed of that either."

I wonder why he doesn't care if his family knows he's bisexual, when he does care if they know he doesn't want to be a doctor. Maybe because the doctor thing is important to him and the rest isn't?

"It's late. I should go." Levi stands, stretches. His shirt pulls up, showing me his pale, taut skin, and the dark trail of hair the leads under his jeans.

"Turn off the light and get into the goddamned bed, Levi."

He grins, familiarity in his eyes, and I know he's smiling not so much because I'm asking him into my bed, but because he remembers saying the same thing to me that night in the hotel. It's not a look I ever expected to get from Levi.

"I can't keep up with you. One minute you look uncomfortable to be around me, you're shy and a little closed off like the kid I knew growing up, and the next you turn into a bossy motherfucker ordering me around."

I can't keep up with myself either. It's true—one moment I'm the younger brother's friend with the secret crush, and the next I'm the experienced Toby who tries to tell himself Levi is just another guy. "My brain hurts too much to dissect it right now."

He toes out of his shoes. I don't turn away as he unbuttons his pants and pulls them down until he's standing there in tight, black boxer briefs and his shirt. He's hard, that's obvious, and even though I am too, I also feel like my whole world might explode. I'm not sure I have it in me to do anything to relieve our erections right now.

His shirt comes next, and yeah, I'm still watching. Levi hits the light, giving us darkness. The bed shifts as he lies behind me, and then we both go to sleep.

CHAPTER EIGHTEEN

I wake up with Levi's arm wrapped around me, his warm breath on my neck. There's a minute where I just lay here, savoring it. The feel of a hard, muscled body against me, the fact that it's this guy in particular. That he came here to seek me out. Maybe it shouldn't, but it makes pride swell in my chest.

That's about when the hangover catches up with me, nausea churning my gut.

"I think I'm going to die." My head feels like there's a bass pounding inside of it.

"I still like the smell of your soap," he responds.

"You remember that?"

"Yeah."

Even though he can't see my face, I smile. "I bought a case of it."

A loud laugh falls out of Levi's mouth and right into my ear, making the bass get louder. "Oh shit. Don't do that. My head is killing me. I need to take something." Rolling over, I sit on the edge of the bed, but then pause before going any further.

"I need some coffee or something. Can I make some?" Levi asks.

I nod, stand, and then say, "Yeah. If there's a guy out there with dark hair, tattoos and piercings, it's my roommate Xavier. If there's someone else out there, Xavier must have brought a guy home last night. I'll be back in a minute."

There's a pair of sweats on the floor, so I pick them up and pull them on. It's not until I make it to the bathroom that I realize I didn't tell Levi where the coffee or anything is. He'll figure it out, though. Before doing anything else, I grab some pain medicine from the cabinet and take two with a handful of water, then piss, wash my hands, and brush my teeth before stumbling to the kitchen.

"Hey." I plop down at the table and see Levi standing next to the coffee pot in a pair of jeans. His brown hair is mussed, like someone had their hand knotted in it. If I hadn't felt like crap, that would have been me. Or hell, maybe I did muss his hair but I don't remember doing it.

"Is it bad that I'm enjoying this? I mean, you had to see me hungover, it's only fair that I see you that way, too."

"There's the Levi I know!" As soon as I say it, I wish the words back. He's going through enough, and I didn't want to remind him of it. But Levi just chuckles at my lame attempt to turn the subject away from me.

"Cups here?" He points to a cabinet. I nod and then stand.

"Sit down," he tells me. "I got it. I didn't get you a birthday present, so I can get you coffee."

Falling back to the chair, I watch him move around my kitchen, comfortable as ever.

"How do you like it?" he asks.

"Black."

"That's gross. It's bitter that way." He sets the cup in front of me, then looks in the fridge, pulls out Xavier's creamer. "Will he mind? I can buy some more."

"It's fine." I wave him off. Levi makes his coffee and then sits at the small table with me, sipping his drink. Maybe wishing he had a newspaper to read and bacon and eggs in front of him.

I should probably say something, but I don't know what, so I drink some coffee and pretend I haven't slipped back into "I slept in the same bed as Levi fucking Baxter" mode and that this isn't a big thing. If we're going to do this, I have to come at it like Levi is just some guy I met. It can't be about anything more than that.

"I didn't know you had a roommate," he says after a few minutes.

"There's probably a lot about each other that we don't know."

He nods. "True."

A noise comes from down the hallway. Xavier stumbles out of his room in his boxer briefs.

"I smelled coffee." He rubs his eyes as he comes into the kitchen. Levi watches him, turning as Xavier pours himself a cup and then looks in the fridge for his creamer. It always takes Xavier at least one cup to wake up and act partially human.

"Dude, am I out of creamer?"

Levi's still watching him, which is understandable—Xavier's ass in underwear is a thing of beauty—but I also have the urge to grab Levi's face and turn it toward me.

"It's on the counter, man," I tell him. "You missed it." He looks up at me, then his eyes shift to Levi, noticing him for the first time.

"What's up?" Xavier nods at him, pushes his hair behind his ears and looks away. "I'm a prick until I've had my coffee. I'd talk but then you'll just think of me as Toby's asshole roommate, and you're pretty sexy, so I don't want you to think I'm a douche."

After this statement, he doctors his coffee and stumbles back to his room. Yep, that's my roommate.

"He's um…"

When Levi doesn't finish his sentence, I do it for him, but probably not with words he would choose. "Going to get his ass kicked." I'm down with Xavier's quirks but not so much with him calling my guest sexy.

And…I totally need to simmer down on possessiveness here.

"Well, hell. Look at you. There's steam coming out of your ears, Toby. You jealous because he thinks I'm sexy? I mean…look at me. You know I am."

I grab a napkin off the table, ball it up and throw it at him. "Fucker. And I'm not jealous." I'm totally fucking jealous.

Levi takes a drink of his coffee before tossing the napkin back at me. "Good. You don't have to be. He's not my type."

Does that mean I am? Is that what he's saying? I mean, obviously I turn him on in some ways because I've had him, but that was just sex. Still. "Men in general used to not be your type."

"But they are now. Obviously. Just like you're my type."

My pulse goes from normal to Mach speed in three seconds flat. "Are you saying you want to have sex with me again?"

He shrugs. "I'm saying what I'm saying. Didn't we discuss this last night? I distinctly remember mentioning sleeping together."

He did, but last night I was drunk. Today I'm sober and in my right mind. It's too early and I'm too hungover for this, but still I answer with, "I thought it would be smarter to go with the friends thing. You know, because your brother is my best friend and I'm pretty intertwined with your family."

Levi leans forward, elbows on his knees, and looks at me, questions in the deep brown orbs of his eyes. "I think that's a shitty reason. And have you ever had sex with the same guy twice?"

I drop my head to the chair's back and look at the ceiling. It was weird having this conversation with the guy who used to threaten me with wedgies when I was a kid. "Why does that matter?"

"Humor me. Otherwise I'll call you T-Rex again."

"I'll kick your ass. And can you really call someone that after they've been inside you?"

That makes him sit back. He crosses his arms over his chest, not looking quite as cocky as he did a second ago.

"Good point. Now answer the question."

But I don't want to, and I don't want to think about why.

"Come on, you know something about me that no one else in the world knows. You can't tell me who you've slept with? You know me—I won't shut up until you tell me. I like getting my way."

I laugh and it makes a pain shoot through my head. Leaning forward, I rub my temples. "No shit on getting your way, and don't make me laugh." He doesn't respond, but I know he'll eventually keep bugging me until I do what he says. That's Levi. "One guy... It was only a few times though, spread out over a couple months."

"Wow..." He looks surprised by that answer. "Serious?"

"No. I told you I've never been serious about anyone."

"I didn't think so."

"Fuck you."

"Hey! Not because someone wouldn't be into you. I'm just saying I have a theory when it comes to you, that's all. Why'd you guys stop sleeping together?"

There isn't a part of me who wants to do this with him. Not now, not ever. "I don't know. I just told him I was over it." I push away from the table and stand. "I need to take a shower to see if it helps me feel better. See ya in a few."

And somehow I have a feeling I just told him something he already guessed, and that he doesn't like the answer.

CHAPTER NINETEEN

I take a long time in the shower. By the time I get out my fingertips are raisins but I feel a whole lot more human than I did when I got in. The alcohol really hit me last night. I'll be sweating it out all day.

After wrapping a towel around my waist, I cross the hall for my bedroom. When I open the door, Levi's lying on his back on the bed watching me. "I thought you drowned."

"Considered trying to make that happen. You comfortable?"

"Yes. Do you have a problem with it?" He winks and I just roll my eyes at the bastard. "I considered getting in the shower with you. That would have been a lot more comfortable, but you're being weird. For someone who supposedly used to jack off to thoughts of me, you don't seem to want me around all that much. Or at least not naked. I think my feelings are hurt."

"Who left? Maybe we could have screwed our way through Christmas vacation?" I cock a brow at him and Levi flinches. "And you don't have your feelings hurt. You just want to hear me say I want you. You've always had a big head like that." And honestly, that makes sense with what's going on in his life. Maybe he *needs* to hear something like that more than he *wants* to.

I walk over to my dresser and open the drawer, which puts my back to him. "You know I want you." I shrug. "Everyone wants you."

Plucking out a pair of black briefs, I drop my towel and pull them on.

"You have a nice ass."

I'd be lying if I didn't admit my lips pull into a smile. When I don't respond, Levi continues, his voice a husky, sexy rasp. "You're different."

"You're different, too."

"I like you this way. Confident. You've always been a little more quiet and shy, and when you did talk, it was usually some kind of joke."

Because laughing made it easier to be around him. Hell, to be around anyone. "That's what happens when you grow up. People change." My drawer gets off track when I try to close it. I rattle it a second, but then don't feel like screwing with it and open the bottom drawer for jeans, which I put on. "Maybe that's what happened to you. You grew up and you changed. Nothing wrong with that." Looking over my shoulder, my eyes catch his. I see the turmoil there, the confusion. "This doctor thing, it's not a big deal, man. That's not the kind of profession you go into if you don't have a love for it."

Levi huffs, pushes up and sits on the edge of the bed. His right leg bounces rapidly as though it's trying to get somewhere. "In a way, I do have a love for it. I respect it. But it's hard to give up on something I've worked so hard on. To ignore the money my parents have put out and the scholarships I've been given." He puts his hand on his leg as if to stop the bouncing. It doesn't stop—the mattress is shaking. "You and Chris didn't see the pressure Dad put on me. I know Chris thinks it's all fucking perfect in my world, but it's not. Dad accepted that Chris isn't going to follow in his footsteps. There's a freedom in that. It's always meant the goddamn world to my dad that I'd become a doctor. I didn't get the choice."

I watch him for a few moments quietly, letting his words sink in. "You're right," I say finally.

Levi winks. "I know." But then he fidgets, glances away, almost as though he's embarrassed.

"But only about us not understanding the pressure you were under. The rest of it… You can still make whatever changes you want, Levi. I believe that."

The frown on his face says he doesn't agree with me. He doesn't argue though, just asks, "Can we chill today? Do you work or anything? Hell, I don't even know if you have a job."

When I don't answer right away, Levi picks up a sock and throws it at me. Fucker. "So," he says. "Hang out? Job? Are you in there?"

"Just a part-time job at a coffee house. I'm going to be screwed with student loans when I graduate, but it's worth it to me. And no, I don't work this weekend. What do you want to do?" A quiet buzz builds deep inside me, getting more electric by the second. It shouldn't feel this exciting to get the chance to spend the day with him. My reaction almost makes me want to say no, but this doesn't have to be a big deal. I've basically told him I'm willing to give this friends thing a shot.

"Hell, I don't know. We can stay here all day if you want. There's a beer festival, but I'm pretty sure you're not feeling that right now. We can play tourist and go hang out at Pier 39 or something. We're from Oregon so it's not as if we're not used to the dreary grey day and showers."

"Yeah, okay." I shrug. "That sounds cool."

I shove my hands in my pockets, trying to act all business as usual as I watch Levi stand. He pulls a small container out of his pocket, opens it, drops a pill in his mouth and swallows. "Can I borrow a shirt or something?"

I ignore his question and concentrate on breathing because my stomach's just filled with concrete. I can't believe how casually he's popped a pill. Right in front of me. I'm hoping like hell it's a vitamin or ibuprofen or something and not what I think it is.

Levi glances my way and must notice I look freaked out because he says, "I take anxiety medication. It's not a big deal. Don't say anything. My parents don't know."

"It's not a big deal, but they don't know?" Sounds like he's making it a big deal to me.

Levi sighs. "There's a large population of people who take medication for anxiety. I'm one of them. As long as I take it, I stay even. I know enough to make sure I take it. That's all, man."

Logically, I know he's right. Levi's like a thousand-piece puzzle—you know he's going to take a while to figure out. But then when you open the box, you realize they must've mislabeled it and there's actually two-thousand pieces there.

"Shirt?" he asks again. "Or are you trying to make me grungy so you won't want me so much? By the way, I'm still trying to figure out what the problem with that is."

Levi's warm, smooth hand wraps around my wrist when I reach out to shove him. "Cocky motherfucker."

"So I've been told." He gets a wide grin on his face that disintegrates the concrete in my stomach. He's too sexy for his own good.

Jerking out of his grip, I say, "Let go of me so I can get you some clothes. There should be a new stick of deodorant under the sink, so you don't stink me out all day. And a toothbrush and razors. Xavier has what he calls a Post-Bang Survival Kit. You know how some people prepare for the world to end? Xavier stockpiles everything a guy needs the morning after."

A loud laugh jumps out of Levi's mouth. I haven't heard that sound much lately, and I turn around, digging in my dresser so he doesn't see how much I like it.

"That's awesome. Does he have a pre-bang kit, too? I mean, besides the obvious?" he asks.

"Actually, he does. He keeps it in his room. If I'm being honest, I'm a little afraid to know what's in that one."

My reply earns me another laugh from Levi. It's like he's giving me some kind of gift, like Levi's enjoyment is somehow mine, which sends off all sorts of sensors and warnings that I try to shut down. "Here." I toss him a shirt. "Get ready so we can get out of here." And I can get a few minutes alone to figure out what in the hell I'm doing.

CHAPTER TWENTY

"I want to ride the trolley." There's an excited quiver to Levi's voice, as though he can hardly hold it in. His contents are under pressure and if he doesn't find release somehow, he'll explode. He does this sometimes, gets this giddy kind of enthusiasm about the smallest things. It's totally not my gig.

"And I want a million dollars. Or all my student loans paid off."

"I'm serious, Toby. Ride the damned trolley with me."

The frown on my face is automatic, pulling my lips tight. Riding the trolley feels like such a… I don't know. Like a lame thing to do. "You weren't kidding about the tourist thing."

"No, I wasn't. Remember how I like to get my way? Let's go. I looked up where the closest stop is; we need to go right."

When he touches my arm, I swear my skin absorbs some of his enthusiasm. This is all part of his charm, how he pulls people in so easily. And suddenly I'm thinking riding the trolley could be kind of cool…in a cheesy, made-for-TV-movie kind of way.

"Have you ever ridden it?" he asks.

"Nope."

"Why the hell not? We did when we came down here for vacation, before med school. I think Dad was living vicariously through me."

I can see how that would happen. When Levi got accepted at Stanford it was all Dr. Baxter spoke about. It drove Chris out of his mind. I'd been slightly fascinated by the news, because Levi always fascinated me. It's weird to look back and realize that Levi was the only one feeling conflicted by the deal.

"So, anyway, you're too cool for the trolley?" he asks, pulling me from my thoughts.

"Fuck yeah. Too cool for you, too, but I'm making an exception."

"Didn't sound like an exception when you were telling me how you used to jerk off thinking of me. It sure as hell didn't sound that way when you were pounding me."

My foot catches on an uneven spot on the sidewalk, and I stumble forward. The bastard starts laughing his ass off, people looking at us when they walk by.

"I love that I can make you do that. You get flustered and when you do, it makes you clumsy. It's adorable."

On the one hand, I like him thinking I'm adorable as long as it's not in a cute-kid kind of way. On the other hand, "Fuck off. The timing was coincidental."

"No it wasn't."

"Yes it was."

"No—"

"Will you stop it? Jesus, you're like a kid, sometimes." No matter how hard I try to feign annoyance, I can't hold back my smile. Without looking, I know Levi is smiling, too.

"It's a nice change, Toby. I haven't felt like this in too long."

This time it's my heart that stumbles before finding its footing again. *No, no, no.* I can't let the organ in my chest get involved at all when it comes to Levi. He's enjoying himself now, and maybe I'd like to think it's because of me, but it won't last. Things never do.

I'm freaked out that I'll want it to.

I'm so incredibly fucked when it comes to Levi Baxter, and I know it.

***

All day I find myself with my eyes on him, waiting to get a clearer picture of exactly who Levi is. Just as soon as I think one thing, he throws me—the story about his dad, the excitement over the trolley, dealing with anxiety, his worry about becoming a doctor. The more time I spend with him, the more I want to know everything about him. What makes him tick, and what makes him smile? What goes through his head every day and why is it so hard for him to admit he doesn't want to be a doctor? It was easy when I thought I knew exactly who Levi was. Now my image is distorted, but that doesn't stop me from wanting him.

Which yeah, I'm aware makes no sense, but most of the time what people feel doesn't make sense. Not in my opinion.

"How'd you know where I'd be last night?" I ask Levi as we walk through one of the stores on the pier. The place is a mishmash of knickknacks, chimes, pictures and stuffed animals of all things. Levi has to walk behind me instead of next to me as we make our way through the maze of wizards, fairies and strange pig statues.

"This store is weird," he replies, before adding, "I called Chris."

"What the fuck?" My heart drops to my feet as I whip around to look at him.

"Dude, relax. I didn't tell him about our deep, dark secret, even though I don't totally understand why it *is* a secret."

"My sex life isn't other people's business."

"So I'm part of your sex life, huh? Does that mean we get to do it again?" He waggles his eyebrows at me, acting like an idiot.

"Shut up."

"You're smiling."

"No I'm not." I'm totally fucking smiling. The bastard. "What did you say to him?" I move toward the back of the store. The rows don't get any bigger, but Levi finds a way to walk next to me, our arms rubbing against each other as we move. I like the feel of him, and wish we weren't wearing jackets so we'd be skin to skin.

"I just played it off like I didn't know it was your birthday. He said he'd just gotten off the phone with you, and you were going out because you turned twenty-one. I laughed it off and said maybe I'd make the trip to San Fran to give you shit. He told me to leave you alone, and that you were heading to some gay club called Blue Velvet and I wouldn't want to be there anyway. Voila. I'm magic."

"You're an idiot," I say but really my chest is airy and light. Yeah, I've been fighting it, but I've felt good all day because of him. It's like he sucks the negative energy out of a situation. He's such a bright fucking light that you can't fight happiness when he's around. Which makes the fact that I know he's miserable on the inside so much more tragic. Maybe all the bright lights of the world get snuffed out by quiet tragedy nobody sees.

"Do you guys talk on the phone often?" It doesn't seem like they would. Chris never mentions it to me.

"No." Levi shakes his head. "I pretended I had to ask him something about Mom."

I wish I could help them fix their situation—find a way to get them to talk to each other about what they think is truly important. They might realize they have a lot more in common if they did. Words are funny like that, though. They're hard to spit out, hard to let out of your head. Feels so much safer to keep them inside of you. It's that way for me, at least.

"Oh, hey, look at this." Levi puts a hand on my hip. I turn to see what he's looking at, his hand still firmly latched onto me. "It looks like your tattoo. Why'd you get an owl?" he asks.

Reaching out toward the owl figurine he's gesturing toward, I rub my finger over its bulging eyes, touch the bright colors of the feathers. He's right; it does look like my tatt. "I like owls."

"You're a liar. I mean, you might, but there's a reason. You're a thinker, Toby. You wouldn't have picked something to engrave into your skin unless it truly meant something to you."

Shaking my head, I make a move to pull away, but his grip on my side tightens. "You make it sound like you know me so well," I complain.

"I do."

"No you don't."

But really, maybe he does. He's pegged me here.

"I'm starting to," he says. "I think maybe I didn't pay enough attention before. I'm paying attention now. I've given you pieces of me, can't you give me something of you, too?"

His breath whispers across my skin. While one part of me is thinking, *Fuck yeah! Levi is interested in me!* the other is telling me it's an incredible waste of time and to move the hell on.

"Come on," he coaxes. "It's easier to learn who you are than to try to figure out who I am. I'm doing all this shit I don't want to do, T. Talk to me about you. That's the only thing I really want right now."

My muscles go rigid and I ball my hands into fists. He's making this hard and I don't want it to be fucking hard. I want it to be easy. We had sex, he bailed, the end. But then he came back. Most people don't come back. And maybe he's with me just for a weekend or because he doesn't want to focus on his own life, but he's here and sounds honest and raw, like every time he talks to me, he's bleeding for me. And because Levi has always seemed so invincible in the past, I have this strange urge to bleed for him, too, even when I've promised myself I'd never cut myself open for anyone.

"It's stupid," I say.

"And going to school for something you don't want, isn't? Come on, man. That's a bullshit excuse and you know it."

He's right and it's just like Levi to call me out on it.

"Excuse me." A woman squeezes around us, heading toward the front of the store, leaving Levi and I alone in the back. His hand slides down, grips mine and pries my fingers open. I hadn't realized I was still making a fist until he touched me.

"Owls are smart," I tell him. "They represent wisdom. Who doesn't want wisdom to represent them?"

Levi's hand drops away. "Fuck you, Toby. You said we're friends. That's all I'm trying to be. You can't even be real with me."

He takes one step. The need to have him back—to feel him close against me—is sudden and urgent. So now it's me who's reaching out and grabbing. Me demanding he stay close. It's not something I've ever done, not with anyone.

I look into his eyes and try to explain. "It's just…a lot of myths and stuff like that say that owls see the truth. They're spiritual mirrors, for lack of a better term. They're supposed to be able to show us what we fear."

"Ourselves…" His voice is soft. Our sleeves touch as we stand side by side, my hand still holding his wrist. We probably look crazy…or at least a little too intense about a display of fucking owl figures, but still, neither of us moves.

"Yep. The real us." Which is terrifying. Because what if

you see your true self and you don't like what you see? Levi isn't the only person who's scared of who he is. For him, the scary shit is that he feels like he doesn't know himself. For me, it's that I'm scared of what I could become.

"What else?" he asks. "There's more."

There is, and part of me is surprised he wants to know, but the other is excited to share it with him. "Owls are connected to the Greek goddess of knowledge and foresight. It's important to me that I pay attention, that I'm smart about people and my life, ya know? Owls are fascinating, really. They like to avoid the craziness in life. They'd rather be alone."

Levi chuckles quietly. "They'd rather be alone? Hmm…that sounds familiar. Except when you go out for a piece of ass, at least. Other than that, it explains you perfectly."

Nudging him with my arm, I say, "Shut up." But he's right and I know it. "They're also known to be bad omens or a warning of death."

"Okay, so maybe it doesn't fully sound like you…you got an omen of death tattooed on your arm? That's morbid." His lips thin as they stretch into a smile.

"I'm a morbid guy. What can I say?" But yeah, I'm grinning, too. Before he thinks I'm being real, I say, "I'm kidding. That's just a fact about them. The death thing isn't why I got it."

"Didn't think it was," Levi replies. "Maybe I need to connect to my spirit mirror and it can tell me what in the fuck I'm doing with my life." Levi plucks the owl from the glass display. "Now I have a reminder of you when we're apart."

I look at him, pause, almost lose my shit, and then burst out laughing as Levi does the same.

"I'm joking. I use that picture I took of you when you were naked for that. Awesome spank material."

We're both still laughing when we buy his owl and then leave the store.

CHAPTER
TWENTY-ONE

We eat lunch and then walk around a little more. We make our way from the pier and go to Godiva, before browsing the stands in a grassy area where people tell fortunes and sell handmade jewelry. I've loved San Francisco since my first day here. I feel the energy of the city in every part of me, currents of electricity pulsing in my muscle tissue, funneling as deep as the marrow in my bones.

When l applied for school, all I'd known was I wanted to be in a city, and I wanted decent queer and ethnic representation. That's all I'd cared about, but I think part of me had to have known this was the place for me, and today I'm wondering why I don't get out and enjoy the city like this more often. Usually I just go from school, to home, work, clubs, and that's it.

On the way back to my place, Levi doesn't try to get me to take the trolley again, so we jump on a bus and make the quick ride home. Xavier isn't there, but the apartment smells slightly like stale cigarettes so I open the sliding glass door to air it out.

Levi walks to the entertainment center and starts looking through Xavier's games. I watch him, wondering why he's still here and when he's planning on leaving. Not because I want him to go, but because he doesn't really have a reason to stay. Yesterday it was my birthday and then it was late when we got back. Today we hung out but now…what's his reason for staying?

"He cool if you play these?" Levi asks.

"Yeah." I shrug.

Levi pulls a game out, puts it in and then nods toward the grey loveseat. "Come on. I'll kick your ass at Call of Duty."

We spend the next couple hours playing video games and eating chips and dip and red vines from this big-ass container Xavier has on the coffee table.

"He's probably going to come home with the munchies and we ate all his stuff." I put a lid back on the red vines with only a few left in the container. "I'll buy him some more tomorrow."

Levi nods toward the window. "It's raining."

"It's always raining. We got lucky earlier today."

He still doesn't make a move to get up and leave. It doesn't escape my attention that I'm not asking him about what the hell he's doing here. I'm not sure how I feel about that. I watch him run his finger over the seam of the couch, and it hits me that he's feeling insecure about something. That he doesn't want to leave. I don't think his feelings have to do with me. More like he's probably not happy about going back to school and what's been making him so insecure. Levi doesn't like to be insecure.

"Watch a movie with me, Levi."

He cocks his head and looks at me like he's trying to see inside me. It reminds me of our conversation about the owl. I'm thinking a spiritual mirror would come in handy about now, because the reason why I'd want him here for more than just sex is a mystery.

"Okay."

So we order pizza, enough for Xavier in case he gets back, and watch some cheesy horror flick.

It's dark by the time it's over, the only light in the room the glow of the TV. Levi asks, "Can I stay?"

It's the kind of thing I'd always dreamed of hearing him say to me. Everything about him right now, the way he asks the question, the expression in his eyes, should all be a dream come true. Still, for a second I consider saying no. And when I say a second, I mean it's really only a tiny blip in time before I'm saying, "Yes."

"Cool. Can I borrow more clothes and use your shower?" His voice is low, sexy, and a thrum of excitement shoots through me.

"You're a needy bastard, aren't you?" But I push to my feet and head to my room. Levi's right behind me. I throw him a towel, a pair of sweats and a T-shirt, and then fall onto my bed as I wait for him to shower.

For the second time in my life, I'm going to have sex with Levi Baxter. I mean, what else would he be staying for? Yeah, I know he doesn't want to go back to Palo Alto yet, but he's also made it clear he's interested in the friends-who-bone thing. I'm not sure either one of us will be able to pull off any kind of friendship with each other, but for tonight we'll have a little fun, forget about everything else, and this time when we walk away, we'll both be on the same page and know this is over.

The pipes are loud in the apartment so I listen to the clinking, clanking and running water for what feels like forever. Eventually there's a loud rumble that tells me Levi turned the water off. A few minutes later, he opens the door, crosses the hall and makes it into my room only wearing the sweats and holding the T-shirt in his hand. His wet, brown hair hangs over his forehead, making it so he's peering at me through the strands. It's sexy as hell. Heat prickles on my skin as I watch him run a hand through it, pushing it back.

"You're eyeing me like you're ready to jump my bones at any second." He cocks a brow at me because he knows I want him, but he also knows I've been trying to ignore it. Yeah, he really sucks right now. "Should I go raid Xavier's room for the pre-bang kit?"

I feel the smile deep inside me before it makes an appearance on my face. Damn him for making me like being around him. That's not usually something I have to deal with from people in my life. "Shut up and come here."

With his foot, he pushes the door closed, a loud bang echoing through the apartment. "Why don't you ask me nicely?"

I sit up so I'm on the edge of the bed. I wrack my brain trying to think of something creative to say, but it turns out my brain has, for real, turned off, so I listen to my erection and say, "Please come here, Levi."

He drops the shirt and walks over, stopping right in front of me. He smells like soap, *my* soap, the stuff I stocked up on because he liked it. Levi was right. It smells good on someone else's skin. Leaning forward, I lick at his flat stomach, running my tongue over the flesh at the edge of the sweats.

"I bought more of this stupid soap because of you," I say. "Now I see what you meant. I love the way it smells on you."

"I like it when you're horny. You admit stuff you wouldn't say otherwise."

Damn it, he's right. Ignoring that, I kiss his abs, keeping my mouth busy with tasting instead of talking. I run my hand up the back of his legs, palm his ass, and then dip my hands under the sweats to pull them off. Levi grabs my face, tilting it up so I'm looking at him. "No. You got to taste me last time. It's my turn to have my mouth on you."

Brain still off, cock running the show, I lean back and wait. There's not a chance in hell I'm turning down that offer.

CHAPTER TWENTY-TWO

I'm embarrassed to admit my pulse is going crazy as Levi kneels in front me. It's not the typical I'm-about-to-get-head excitement. It's more like the Levi-Baxter-is-on-his-knees-for-me kind.

He's beautiful. He's always been beautiful, but in this moment, wet hair in his face as he works the button and zipper on my jeans, he's fucking incredible.

"Lift up." He swats my leg and I obey him so he can pull down my pants and underwear.

He runs his hands up my bare thighs, and I feel every little wrinkle of his pruned fingers against my sensitive flesh.

"Can I say your skin looks like caramel if I follow with a chaser of, 'And I want to lick it up'?"

Laughter bubbles up from deep in my gut. "Holy shit, you are such an idiot."

"I make you laugh, though."

I hiss when he wraps a hand around me and strokes. "No…surprise…there." He pauses and I finish with, "You've always been funny," before he pumps his hand again.

"Have I? I thought I lost it. Or at least lost being genuine about it and not just playing a role. It feels real again."

Levi doesn't give me time to dissect what he said (not that I want to), before he sucks me deep. A moan pushes past my lips as I sink into the wet cavern of his mouth. He uses his hand at the same time, stroking, licking and sucking like his life depends on it. He's good, like he could win the dick-sucking World Series if there was one. I plunder deep into his mouth, and as I do, he looks up at me through thick lashes, coaxing a strangled moan out of me.

Heat plunges through me, burning my whole body as I savor the feel of his mouth on me, as I tangle my hand in his hair and guide him. Levi groans around me, sending a vibration through me, and it's almost enough to end this before I'm ready. I pull him off and take his mouth with mine.

Our tongues tangle, duel, fight to possess each other's mouths. He tastes like toothpaste. There's a light layer of sweat on his body now, we're making each other so hot. At least I'd like to think I'm making him as wild as he's making me.

I stand up and Levi follows, our mouths still attached. I finish kicking out of my pants as I push his sweats down and out of the way. He rubs against me, his hardness on mine as I squeeze his tight cheeks, pulling him closer.

"Shirt off," he says against my mouth, so I pull away. Levi wraps a hand around both of us, stroking as I rip my shirt over my head.

"That feels good." I shudder, thrust forward, delirious with need.

"It'll feel better in a minute. I can't believe how crazy you make me."

I choose to ignore the part about him not being able to believe he wants me. We fall to the bed, laughing and kissing. I've never really laughed when I was messing around with someone before. It makes all the good stuff I'm feeling even better.

Our bodies are aligned, me on top of him. He's holding onto my ass now as I writhe against him, my tongue deep in his mouth. Pulling back, my lips make a trail down to his neck, and I lave his Adam's apple with my tongue.

"We doing this or not?" He's breathless and I love that I'm making him that way. He's making me the same.

"We are doing it. You want more?"

"I want more," he replies. There's not a chance I'm making him wait. I knock a cup off my bedside table, trying to get into the drawer. Water spills everywhere and Levi laughs. "See? You're clumsy when you're horny."

He squeezes me, kneads my globes. "And you're cocky all the time." Finally my hand wraps around a small bottle, and then a small square package. "Found it. Thank fuck. I thought I was going to have to keep listening to you gloat."

I slide off him, open the condom and roll it down.

"You like me. Don't pretend you don't," he says.

And he's right. That doesn't mean I'm going to admit it. "No I don't."

"Yes you do."

"Why do you like arguing with me so much?" I ask, but

that light feeling in my chest is expanding, growing and swelling so much it makes it hard to breathe, because I like it, too.

"Because it's fun. You're fun. You stopped moving."

"Bossy." I roll him to the side, so his back is to me. Levi bends his top leg in front of him, as I lube my fingers, then myself, before rubbing more lube on him.

The second I push in, I almost lose it and come all over the place. He's a hot, tight cave that I want to live inside. Holding still, I bite the tendon that runs along his neck to keep from embarrassing myself.

When I'm finally under control, I pull out before thrusting forward again. His body is hugging me, so hot and tight. "Damn you feel good."

"You too." Levi grabs my hand and puts it on his dick. "Now take me, Toby."

And I do. Hard. Sweat beads on my forehead, rolls into my eyes and drops down to Levi's neck. Each time I pump my hips, I jerk him off. He's thrusting into my hand and onto my rod at the same time.

It doesn't take long before I begin to feel the familiar burn and tingle. Just as soon as he covers my hand in hot, thick, fluid, I let go, slamming into him as I ride out the best orgasm of my life.

I pull out of him, panting. He has an arm thrown over his face. His spent, flaccid cock rests against his stomach. As I look at him I suddenly feel like I'm choking. Like I can't breathe. I've again had hot, filthy sexy with gorgeous golden boy, Levi Baxter. There's come all over the place, and everything about this, about *him* feels so damn good that I'm not sure how to handle it. "I'll be right back. I'll get something to clean up."

"Huh. Why would you do that? Being messy is the best part." He rolls toward me, throwing a leg over me.

And he's totally right. "You're dirty."

"Dirty is good."

He's right about that, too.

Seems like at least an hour passes as we lie here awake. We don't speak but I swear I hear a quiet whispering happening between us, a soft mumble in the room as our thoughts run through us and make their way into each other.

I can't hear his words, but I know they're there.

"I'm afraid of my dad," Levi suddenly says. "Not because I think he would ever physically hurt us, but because…"

He doesn't finish the sentence. I nod to show him I understand. "I used to wish he was my dad," I admit. "I was afraid of him, too, but I liked that in a way. He's strong and puts out the aura that he knows everything, that there's nothing he can't do." Which is so different than the way I see my dad. People don't fuck with Dr. Baxter. They do what he says. They respect him.

My dad doesn't respect himself.

Levi respects his dad so much, he puts his dad's happiness over his own.

Levi reaches for my hand. When I take it and squeeze his fingers, he says, "I failed a biology test my junior year in high school. I was scared shitless to bring it home. I didn't want to let him down, ya know? I begged the teacher to let me retake it and she said no. I puked on my way home, vomited because of a fucking test, man."

My own stomach clenches up hearing him speak about it. It's not something I ever would have expected out of him. So much of Levi's behavior seems to be so different than what I've always thought.

"I made sure to go home when I knew Chris wasn't there. I knew dad would freak and I was embarrassed because I don't get F's. That's not me."

He shifts on the bed and then I ask, "What happened?"

"He lost it. He was disappointed in me. He knew I was *better* than that, as though one F meant I'd be a failure my whole life. One call from him and my teacher let me retake that test, though. She couldn't say no to him, and I couldn't fail."

I get now what Levi's saying… We're not just talking about that test from years ago. We're talking about his life now.

He can't fail and his dad always wins.

CHAPTER
TWENTY-THREE

It's grey and foggy when I wake up Monday morning.
Looking out the window, the wetness in the air is obvious. My
bones feel the weather like I'm sixty-one instead of twenty-
one. Or hell, maybe not. Maybe I'm just looking for an excuse
to stay under the covers instead of getting up. They smell like
Levi and sex. I had him twice again yesterday before he left—
once with me inside him and the second time with him in my
mouth.

Pulling the blanket over my head, I breathe in, savoring
the warmth; but then my cell starts beeping again and I know
I have to get up and get my ass to school. I head straight for
the shower. My mind runs over the weekend while hot water
flows over my skin. We spent yesterday watching movies and
playing video games between stints of touching each other in
my room, all so Levi could stall and not head back to Palo
Alto, as though staying away means he isn't really in his
second year of med school.

The fucked-up part of the whole situation is that I
enjoyed it way more than I should have. I enjoy Levi in a
different way than I ever have and I don't mean just because

I've had my dick inside him and his mouth around me.

The pipes make their typical banging and clanking sounds as I turn off the water and get out. I shave real quick, brush my teeth and get dressed before heading back to my room to pack up all my shit.

There's a glow from the living room in an otherwise dark apartment, and when I get there, Xavier's sitting on the couch playing a game with the volume muted. "Sucks to be you. I haven't even gone to bed yet and you're already heading out."

"We can't all spend our time blowing shit up."

"Jealous?" Xavier cocks his head and grins at me, laughter in his ice-blue eyes.

"So jealous I can hardly stand it."

He tosses the controller to the couch, the tunnel of light from the TV helping me see him. Eyeliner's smeared under his eyes, giving them smoky shadows. "So your dude finally left last night?"

Shit. I should have known he'd go there. "He's not mine. He's just an old friend who's dealing with some stuff. He doesn't want to face his future and it's like he thinks hanging out with me will keep him in the past."

"Whatever you say. If he needs a distraction and you're not around, tell him to give me a call."

Tightness spreads through my chest, makes my muscles go rigid.

"See? You don't like that thought, do you? Just keeping it real. This is cool. Now that you spent the weekend getting ass, we're getting closer. It's almost like we're friends instead of just roommates."

Yeah if friends talk about wanting to hook up with the same person their friend is screwing. Not that it should matter. Levi and Xavier have a right to do whoever they want. And spending the weekend with Levi didn't change that. "You're crazy. We're still not friends."

Xavier laughs and shakes his head. "I think we are. I just might be getting a handle on you. Wanna chat and help me paint my nails tonight?"

Heading toward the door, I glance over my shoulder at him. "You're an idiot."

"I'm serious, dude. It's chipping and I have a hard time doing my left hand."

It's a legit excuse, but still not something I'm doing. "I work tonight. You're on your own." The door closes a little harder than I mean for it to and the echo feels as though it's vibrating through me. The friend comment bounces around inside me, making that emptiness grow.

No, Xavier and I don't sit around and talk or really hang out much, but we're cool. He makes it sound as though I'm this closed-off douchebag, yet after a weekend of sex, I've suddenly changed.

He's crazy.

Only, he's not the only one who's basically told me I keep a fortress between myself and others. Cherise and Brian obviously feel the same way.

All morning I try to sort through the thoughts crowding my brain. Who cares if I have a lot of close friends? I'm not closed off. My dad is closed off. I do things besides go to school. I meet people, hang out with people, enjoy people. Sure, I may not be an open book, but I'm not the guy who doesn't know how to relate either.

My third and last class of the day I have with Cherise. She steps up beside me as I'm walking from the lecture hall. She opens her mouth to say something, but words suddenly fall out of mine before she gets the chance. "Wanna grab a coffee or something with me? I can get to the coffeehouse a little before I have to clock in."

See? Screw Xavier. I chill with people just as much as the next guy.

"Um...sure. Where did that come from?"

Dude. "What do you mean where did it come from? It's a simple question."

Cherise's brows pull together. "A simple question you've never asked me. I'm just a little surprised, but sure. Let me text Brian and tell him. Which one will we be at?"

"Whitman's." The owner is this really eccentric old dude who's obsessed with Walt Whitman.

She texts Brian as we head out of the building and into the gloomy day. I slide my beanie over my head, then my hoodie over that. Cherise is already in a jacket as we make our way down the street and to Whitman's.

"How long have you worked here?" she asks when I pull the door open for her.

"Um..." I push my hoodie down and pull the beanie off. "Since about midway through freshman year. It's just part time, but it helps. I was lucky they let me come back after the summer." There's movement out of my peripheral. "Wanna grab that table and I'll get a drink? What do you want?" It's always pretty packed in here. Even more so when they do poetry readings. I'll come down sometimes and listen to them read, or do my work here. The walls are covered with pages from books, words, and pictures of authors. It's relaxing.

"Just a small mocha is fine. I'm already too wired. Coffee makes it worse."

I chuckle because yeah, I can see that from her. It doesn't take me long to get our drinks. When I join her at the table, she asks, "Did you have a good weekend?"

Thoughts of the pier and owls and, yeah, sex fill my head and I answer honestly. "Yeah, it was cool. A little unexpected, but cool."

"Why unexpected? You mean us going to Blue Velvet with you? I feel bad if we pushed our way into your night."

Well that was nice of me. I made her feel bad for trying to be friends with me. "No, no. Not that. It was cool. I'm glad you guys went. This guy I grew up with goes to Stanford Medical School. He showed up. I've known him since I was ten, but never really spent much time with him alone. He's my friend's brother, and he ended up staying, so it was just weird."

"A doctor, huh?" She winks at me but instead of eliciting the kind of reaction from me I assume she wants, it just makes me a little sad.

"It's not what he wants, though. He feels trapped. Obligated. Like he's invested so much into it he doesn't have a choice."

"Wow…" Cherise takes a drink of her coffee. Realizing I'm just letting mine sit, I do the same. "That sucks. Medicine isn't the kind of field you want to go into if your heart isn't in it."

"Well, I do know Levi respects it. His dad is a doctor. It's what he used to want, but I think...hell, people change. Who the fuck really knows what they want when they're eighteen and heading to college? It's hitting him now, and then he feels bad because it's such an honorable thing to do— save lives the way his dad does. I guess he feels like he should still want that."

That's the difference between Levi and myself. The one thing I really do know is what I want from my future. I want to do something I love, not waste away the way Dad does...the way Levi might. Dad never gave a shit what I did. That always bothered me, like it meant he didn't care, but then I think of Levi and how his father wants so much for him to follow in his footsteps, and I wonder if that might be worse.

"Anyway," I say, "I don't know why I went off like that. How are your classes going?"

"All right. I'm struggling a little, if I'm being honest."

"I can help if you want. I mean, I'm sure you'll be fine, but if you want to talk through it, I'm around."

Cherise smiles so bright I think it has the ability to take all the greyness out of San Francisco. "That would be awesome, Toby. Thanks."

My phone vibrates against my thigh. Leaning back, I pull it out of my pocket to see Levi's number on the screen. **Hey, T. How was your day?**

I stare at the screen for a few moments and listen to my heart thud. Sometimes people let the little things go. They don't ask how someone's day is, or talk to them over dinner, letting silence take the place of conversation. Silence hurts sometimes. It always did at home. It's such an easy fucking thing, asking about someone's day, but looking at Levi's text, I'm beginning to wonder if maybe it isn't small at all.

"Must be the doc. You're smiling."

"I'm not smiling," I reply.

"Yes you are."

"No, I'm—what the hell is it with people wanting to argue with me?"

She follows that line of conversation instead of finishing our previous one, so I don't have to admit that I might have been smiling.

CHAPTER
TWENTY-FOUR

The whole week is crazy busy. We have an employee out sick so I pick up some extra hours at work. Cherise takes me up on my offer and comes with me to the coffeehouse to do homework a few days. She stops by when I get off or goes in early with me. Levi and I have been texting every day. Nothing big, just talking about school and porn and whatever else we can think of that doesn't really matter.

On Friday the first text comes earlier in the day than the ones from the rest of the week. At first I think it's going to be Chris instead of Levi, since Chris's time zone is three hours ahead, but as soon as I glance at the screen, I realize I'm wrong.

Want some company this weekend? I can come down tonight if you don't have plans.

Crazy how a couple sentences can cause a colossal storm in my head. Excitement's in there. I know that. I want to spend the weekend with Levi again. But there's confusion too, because I don't really see where this can go. If he wants to get laid, he can do that in Palo Alto as easily as he can here.

Guilt's part of the turmoil, too. Every time I'm with Levi on the down low, I feel like I'm betraying Chris, but telling Chris his brother and I are fucking doesn't make a whole lot of sense either. Why fight with my best friend because of sex?

Honestly, there might be a small amount of sadness, too. I have something I've always wanted—Levi wanting to spend time with me—but I'm sure his reasons are all about the past and don't include any hope for the future.

Don't lose your shit, T. It's cool if you say no.

I don't want to say no to him. But why? Am I just one of those people who can't turn Levi down? One of those people like my dad who'll end up needing and depending on one person, only to have them up and disappear.

Yeah, all this is a shit-storm in my head. But still. A big *yes* teases at the tips of my fingers, wanting to be typed out.

Stop thinking. You're going to drive yourself crazy. Let me come hang out with you.

Staring at the text, I realize how well he knows me. He knows me in ways I didn't think he did. Levi can see me sitting here driving myself fucking crazy over something I don't need to lose it about.

But maybe I've already lost the battle. He can read me in ways that should make me run for cover. And I'm still going to say yes.

My fingers tap across the screen. **Yeah, yeah you can come.**

I just have to keep things light. If I keep my distance, everything will be fine.

***

We spend the weekend hanging around the apartment, doing homework (he has a shit-ton of work), playing games, watching movies, and having sex. It's not a bad gig. I could probably get pretty used to it, but then Sunday evening rolls around and Levi grudgingly heads back to school.

The next week is spent pretty much like the last one—school, work, hanging out with Cherise and Brian, and texting Levi. Only the tone of the texting changes slightly.

It's Tuesday when he demands, **Tell me about grape jelly.**

Umm, it's made of grapes? I reply, but I know what he means. We made sandwiches this weekend, and I can't eat grape jelly without thinking about her.

Ur funny. Tell me. I'll tell you something about me.

What if I don't want to know anything about you? But I do, I really fucking do.

Aww. I'm crushed. Tell me.

I shove my phone in my pocket, because my break is over. When I get off work, on my walk home I read the last text he sent. **Final Jeopardy music's playing in my head till you answer. Thanks for that.**

It's dark and sprinkling, yet I still keep my cold hands out of my pockets and in the chilly air to text back. **She loved grape jelly. It was the last thing she made me.**

I don't want to remember, but I do now. I remember how I'd gotten up for school like normal that morning. How she made me a sandwich, and I left, only she didn't show up after school and she wasn't home when I got back. I was alone and scared and felt so fucking left behind. I never saw her again.

He doesn't ask who *she* is, knowing it's my mom. **I'm sorry.**

No reason to be. It happened. But I appreciate the sentiment. The urge is there, playing at my emotions, wanting me to tell him more. Wanting to say to someone that I'm so fucking pissed at her for leaving, that I've always wondered why. That I feel like she might have stayed with Dad if it wasn't for me and then he'd be a whole lot happier. **I gotta go. Home. Hitting the sack.**

Wait. That one word comes back almost instantly, like he had it typed out waiting for me to tell him I'm running and just had to hit send. And then my phone rings. *Answer it, don't, answer it, don't* plays tug-of-war with me but then...I hit Talk.

"I had a major exam last year," he says into my ear. "All I did was study. I hardly ate or slept. The longer I studied, the more convinced I became I'd fail. Me, fucking fail. It was like that incident from high school all ever again. I'd only failed one test in my life, Tobias, and my dad fixed it for me. I know for a lot of people it's hard to understand the overwhelming fear in that, but for me, the thought of failing, of screwing up makes me crazy. My brain gets impossible to shutdown, so yeah, I was freaking out. My headaches got bad, and that wasn't the first time I'd gotten them. When I did sleep I'd wake up in a cold sweat. The day before the test I locked myself in my room, scared to leave because if I didn't leave that damned apartment, I couldn't take that exam. If I didn't take it, I couldn't fail. If I couldn't fail, everything would be okay."

I jump when a car speeds by blasting music. My heart's going as crazy as Levi's telling me his brain did.

"That's when I knew I had to do something. I went to the doctor—didn't use my insurance because if Dad found out there would be questions—and I came away with a prescription for anxiety meds. It's something I knew I should have done before. As soon as the episodes started months earlier, I recognized them for exactly what they were."

"I'm sorry," comes out automatically. I want to say something more, maybe something that would hopefully comfort him, but all I can think about is Levi locking himself in his room, scared to come out. It makes me wonder if he was struggling with it Christmas break when I saw him hiding out beside his house.

"Thanks, man." His reply is a whole lot better than the one I gave him when he told me he was sorry. "Thanks for telling me about your mom."

Dropping back against the building, I close my eyes. What I just told him is nothing, fucking nothing compared to what Levi revealed to me. He's so much stronger than he realizes. "What I said...it doesn't matter."

"Yeah it does. If it means something to you, it matters. People are always comparing their shit—'This happened to me and it's worse or better than what happened to you'. Really, you can't compare experiences. We all live different lives. Your mom making you sandwiches with grape jelly and then leaving matters to you and that's okay. You told me. I know stuff like that's hard for you, and the fact that you said it matters to me."

It gets harder and harder to breathe. My lungs are in a vise-grip getting squeezed tighter and tighter. He's going to make this hard; he's already making it so fucking hard. When Levi realizes it's okay, that he doesn't have to go to school for something he's not sure about, when he realizes he doesn't have to have all the answers, he's not going to need me.

"Now, you can get off the phone and pretend to go to bed. I just wanted to say that to you."

And then Levi hangs up on me, and I continue standing on the sidewalk, even more confused than I was before.

CHAPTER
TWENTY-FIVE

Friday morning he again asks if he can come up, and this time my "yes" comes a whole lot faster. We don't talk about his anxiety or med school or my mom or anything else. He does his massive amount of work and we screw and eat and play games. The next week is the same, followed by the one after.

We fall into this strange pattern. Strange because it's normal and natural and yeah, scares the shit out of me, because I know what we're doing is temporary. Levi's working his way through the maze in his head and once he's out of it we'll be those same two people who lived in Coburn together who had nothing in common. Two people who wouldn't have to lie to their friends and family when they spend time together.

Every once in awhile, he'll ask me random questions—things about what Chris and I used to do, or stuff about school, or how I came to love English. It's easier to talk to him about real things when I don't have to look him in the eyes. It's as though I trick myself into thinking I'm just going over memories in my own head rather than sharing them with someone else.

It's about four weeks after my birthday, four weeks of weekends with Levi and texts during the week. The sun teases us, peeking through the March clouds as I sit outside the coffeehouse with Cherise, Brian, and one of Brian's friends from his frat.

My phone's clutched tightly in my hand, the buttons digging into my palm as my brain is sidetracked with thoughts of where in the hell Levi is. It's the first Friday since we started hanging out that I haven't gotten the text asking me if he can come for the weekend.

"Hey, it's Toby, right?" The chatter of the people around me quiets at the new voice intruding into our conversation— or their conversation since I'm too busy staring at my phone to talk.

Using my hand, the one still holding my fucking cell, I shield my eyes from the sun. It's the sexy guy from Blue Velvet who wanted to take me home. "Hey, man. What's up?"

"Not much, just enjoying the sunshine while it lasts. How about you?" His eyes are filled with questions, the same kind he had the night we met.

"Hanging out, having coffee. Wanna sit down?" At my words, Brian pulls over a chair from the other table, but Seth shakes him off.

"No, I can't. I have somewhere I need to be. I'm around later though if you want to hang out...?" Seth lets the question hang in the air, and my skin pricks with possible interest.

I should. Why not? It's not as if Levi and I are exclusive. Hell, who knows what he's got planned this weekend since he doesn't seem to be coming here. I want to play it like I don't give a fuck, but the thought is like a virus, making me uneasy and slightly sick. "I can't... I have something I gotta do."

Seth grins, showing a dimple under his mouth. "I gotchu. Just thought I'd try. See you around."

The second he's out of range, Cherise turns to me. "Interesting development. You said no because of the doctor, right?"

"He's not a doctor." Which is totally not an answer and just to be sure I don't have to give one, I take a drink of my coffee. But then as though it acts on its own accord, my mouth opens and I ask, "Plus, how do you know I'm still hanging out with him?" It's not like I share my sex life with her.

"Dude," Brian's friend interrupts. I don't know the guy's name. "I only hang out with you when I'm with Brian and I know you're boning the same guy on the regular. It took me three months of doing that before I realized I had a girlfriend. Sounds to me like you have a boyfriend."

His words make me feel itchy even though there's not a damn reason for it. I've never had a boyfriend in my life, never really wanted one and I don't have one now. They're all staring at me like they're waiting for some kind of reply. Brian's smirking, but Cherise has her "mom" face on so I know it's killing her not to ask me a million questions as though she has all the answers and can make it better. She thinks I'm sad, lonely, but I'm not.

This is all feeling way too "let's sit in a circle and discuss your feelings" for me, so I push to my feet. "I'm going to head out. I'll see you guys next week."

My answer obviously disappoints Cherise. She reaches

out and squeezes my hand. I return the squeeze, but then leave them and head home. The more I walk, the more I'm thinking about Levi and how he came every fucking week to the point that I started to depend on it, only for him to suddenly bail without a word. I don't know why it surprises me. It's not like I didn't know this would happen, but it keeps eating away at me, gnawing at my bones as though they're a last meal.

It was stupid to get used to spending time with him. I'm not sure how I let myself get to this point, but it's becoming more and more clear that's what happened. The blame for that lies solely on me.

By the time I get to the apartment, the sun's gone and there's a light mist of rain wetting my skin, which yeah, totally matches my mood. I try to push the door open, but it's locked, so I have to dig my keys out of my pocket.

The strong smell of weed and a hot-boxed apartment burns my nose the second I open the door. Fucking Xavier. I'm not in the mood for it today. Only it's not just him. Levi's sitting on the small couch with him, pipe in his hand. Their two bodies are so close they touch in a room full of smoke, and suddenly it's not the pot that's burning up, it's me.

CHAPTER
TWENTY-SIX

My body temperature shoots up. The burn of the lighter sizzling and popping on the weed scorches my insides.

"So you come without calling now?" As soon as I've asked the question, I'm thinking maybe he's not even here to see me. There's a little nugget of sense inside me that knows that isn't true, but my stupid-ass ego crushes it.

Levi turns to look at me, Xavier's pipe still in his hand. "I cut out early. I knew you were still in class, so I just came down." When I don't say anything his tone changes into one that sounds kind of hurt. "You had no problem with me being here any other weekend. I didn't know that hinged on a text in the morning."

There are a hundred reasons why walking in and seeing him getting high with Xavier is a problem for me, but I think it's jealousy that's riding me hardest. If it wasn't for me, Xavier would totally want to fuck Levi. He's made that obvious. And it's not like Levi and I are in a serious relationship. Why shouldn't he screw Xavier if both of them are into it?

But as I squint through the smoke and see the glaze over Levi's dark brown eyes, I realize worry might be crowding out my jealousy. Levi isn't a waste case. He's *somebody*. He'll always be somebody. He might not be happy there, but he was smart enough and dedicated enough to be in Stanford fucking Medical School. But now he's skipping class to smoke weed and play video games with Xavier?

"So that's your plan? Skip school, maybe fail out so making choices about your future doesn't have to happen? Brilliant." I toss my backpack to the table.

"Fuck you, Toby," Levi says in unison with Xavier's "That's my cue to bail." He grabs his pipe from Levi's hand and goes out the door.

The swirls of smoke in the room start to disappear; they part and twist away so I can see Levi more clearly through them. There's something there in his hazy eyes— disappointment and hurt.

"You can be a real asshole sometimes, you know that?" He pushes to his feet and heads for the door.

Suddenly I'm not made up of anger and jealousy anymore. Not even blood and muscle and bones. My entire being transforms into desperation. I don't want him to go. *Stay, stay, stay*, takes over my breath and my heartbeat. It's scary and fucked up and I want it gone, but not as much as I want to touch him. I reach over, my fingers hardly curling on the bottom of his hoodie, before he goes out the door. There's not a chance I'm letting go. I clutch that small piece of fabric between my fingers and I tug, trying to get him closer.

"Fuck..." I breathe. "I'm sorry. I didn't mean to be a dickhead." But he doesn't move, doesn't leave the doorway.

"I shouldn't have brought school into it, man. I shouldn't have accused you of trying to fail out. I...I know you better than that." Especially after what he shared with me about his anxiety.

"Why did you?" he asks. "Actually a better question is why do you give a shit if I'm in this apartment with Xavier? *Why* does it matter, Tobias? What's the reason?"

He never calls me that. It's always Toby or T. That's not what makes my thoughts stumble, though. I know what he's doing, what he wants me to say. Levi wants to hear that I'm a jealous bastard.

Maybe his reason has to do with whatever he's going through. He feels like shit about himself, so he needs to hear that he's still the same Levi he always was. That people want him. That I'd probably tear the fucking world apart if Xavier touched him. Those aren't things I know how to force myself to say.

"For someone who loves words so much, you suck at using them when it really matters." There's a smile in his voice and it makes one stretch across my face. It's weak and I'm taking the easy way out that he's offering, but I'll have to take on the bigger battle another day.

Pulling on his hoodie again, I say, "It's been a shitty day." Because I thought he wasn't coming. "I have a crazy amount of work to do. You're welcome to hang out while I do it."

Not "Please stay". Not "I don't want you to go". I choose "You're welcome to stay". He's right about me. I suck at words.

It's official. I'm exactly who I never wanted to be,

exactly what I'm angry at my dad for. I'm the guy who can't open my mouth and say any fucking thing that matters. I'm him.

For a good two hours, Levi and I work almost silently at my kitchen table. My hands start cramping I've been writing for so long. My back aches from being hunched over the table, my left arm bent around my paper and my right hand holding the pencil on it. I don't know why I always write like that, as though I have to shield my words from prying eyes when, in reality, no one probably gives a shit what I'm doing. I guess it goes hand-in-hand with why I can't write first drafts or notes on my laptop. There's something more intimate about pen and paper and for some reason, I need that when I'm working.

Levi's been lost in his own work as well, and for the first time in a while, I glance over at him, see his head down as he studies the paper he's scrawling on.

Only it's not biology or chemistry or whatever the hell else he has to do. He's drawing. A really fucking amazing drawing of a guy with his arm curled around a paper, his hand busily writing. My face isn't in the picture, just my arms and hands and paper. Me. He drew me, beautifully sketched lines and pencil shadings. Seeing it makes my chest feel full, almost like my lungs and ribs don't fit anymore. They're being pushed out by this feeling Levi's giving me without knowing it.

"You're an artist," sneaks past my lips.

Levi's head snaps up at my words, his cheeks a light shade of pink. He shakes his head and wrinkles his nose. "I'm not an artist. I draw sometimes, that's all."

"That's crazy good, Levi. It looks like my hands and arms."

"They are your hands and arms." He winks at me flirtatiously, but I can tell he's a little uncomfortable with the praise.

I scoot my chair closer to him and study what he's done. He's incredibly talented. Yeah doing his schoolwork probably would have been a better way to spend his time right now, but I can't help but be awed by what he created. "You're amazing."

He brushes his thumb back and forth over my arm, both our eyes watching the motion, and I wonder if, like me, he's marveling at the different tones of our skin and how beautiful they look together.

"I had a good muse."

The urge to make a sarcastic comment about his line being cheesy is there, but I can't make the words come out, because I like him thinking of me that way. "I was jealous," I tell him. "Earlier. When I walked through the door and saw you here. I don't know why. Sorry."

Levi nods, his tongue tracing his bottom lip. "I know. You're not as good at hiding as you think you are. Not from me."

He probably wants words here, words I don't have because I still don't know if this is real.

Tilting my head to the side, I look at him, lean in and cover his mouth with mine, because the physical connection between us is definitely real. And easy. My tongue explores every spot I've come to learn and love in his mouth, wanting to take him all in. He needs to shave and his scruff rubs against my face, and I legit think that kissing Levi Baxter might be the best thing in the world. "I want you," I say against his mouth. Somehow the words are easier to say with my mouth close to his and his heavy, eager breath against my skin.

"Then take me." He gets up and runs to my room as though this is a game. I'm following right behind him, willing to play and do whatever he wants.

We get to my room and we're both stripping out of our clothes. His long, lithe, fair-skinned body calls to me. I want to cover it with my own. I want to see us through his artist's eyes—the artist I didn't know was living inside him. And I want to see what he would create if he drew something that shows the two of us.

We fall to the bed, Levi on top of me. His pubic hair tickles my hand as I wrap my fist around the root of his erection and start to stroke him off.

He's working his jaw as he thrusts into my grip, holding himself over me. "Not just me," he says, practically grinding his teeth. "Do both of us together."

And so I do. Reaching over, I grab the lube and squirt some into my hand before wrapping it around both of our erections together. My hand slides up and down our rock-hard dicks, and Levi keeps pumping, keeps thrusting into the cave of my fingers with sharp, practiced slides of his hips.

My balls get tight, but I keep stroking and he keeps riding it out. "If we don't stop this real quick, I'm not going to make it inside of you."

He smiles down at me and fuck, this whole goddamned thing would be a whole lot easier if Levi wasn't so beautiful both inside and out.

"That's okay. We can do that later." He shoves harder, snaps his hips quicker, making me squeeze tighter. And then Levi calls out, comes in two long spurts up my chest and into my belly button. My orgasm comes along right after his. I let loose, my spunk mixing with his in artwork all over my body.

CHAPTER TWENTY-SEVEN

Levi doesn't text on Fridays the next few weeks, but I still know he's coming. It's a whole lot easier to pretend that I'm not getting attached than to think about what our weekends together mean and what might happen in the future. So I do a lot of pretending.

He's been drawing more often, which is pretty cool to see. When I watch him, I can tell he likes drawing more than he admits. It makes him feel good about himself—it's obvious in the way he concentrates and the way he holds his body when he's creating. In the pride he hides in his eyes when he finishes something.

Close to a month after he drew me at the table, we're naked in my bed, the bitter taste of him still in my mouth after having pleasured him.

"I have to go meet Cherise in a few hours. She needs my help with something from school." He shivers when I run my thumb over his nipple.

"Check you out, Mr. Know It All, tutoring people from class and shit. You grew up, left Coburn and now you're the man. Got people begging for your help at school, me jonesing for your dick. You used to think I was the golden boy. Look who's golden now?" Levi cocks a brow at me and I pinch his nipple. "Ouch! You asshole! That hurts." He shoves my hand away, but then grabs it and puts it right back on his chest.

"Shut up. I'm not golden anything. That's still you. You're still Mr. Fucking Perfect to the world."

"Aww, so you admit I'm perfect, huh? See, I knew you liked me more than you were letting on. Now that you've finally had me, you can't get enough of my perfect ass. Don't worry. I understand that I'm irresistible."

"You're a cocky bastard is what you are." I try to pinch him again, but Levi's too fast. He grabs my wrist, pushes and rolls so he's on top of me. My legs are thrashing and I'm pulling and fighting him the whole time, but it's hard to do much damage when I'm laughing too hard to breathe.

He grabs my other wrist, holding my arms over my head. Somewhere along the line I get hard and he does too as we keep wrestling and thrusting against each other.

"Look who's on top again," Levi teases. He pulls one of my arms down and under his knee; the other hand still holds my right wrist as he tweaks my nipple the same way I did to him.

"Ouch. You don't want to be on top and you know it. That's the only reason I'm letting you stay there right now."

"Letting me, huh?" He cocks a brow and thrusts against me, then tries to tickle my side. The sound of his phone ringing breaks through our game.

Levi looks at the table by my bed. "It's my mom."

"Don't answer."

He gets a mischievous grin. "I'm gonna answer it."

It's stupid but my pulse starts rapping a crazy beat. "I just gave you head, and we're naked in bed, where I thought we'd get off again. Don't answer a call from your mom."

"You're embarrassed. She can't see through the phone. You can even jerk me off while I talk to her." He reaches over. Fighting him, I try to get to the phone before he answers it but Levi tugs it away, hardly able to get out the "hello" he's laughing so hard.

Yeah, it is embarrassing. I'll admit that. He rolls off me and settles in beside me on the twin. I try to get up, but Levi pulls me back down.

"What are you laughing at?" Elaine asks—I'm close enough to him that I can hear her speak.

Levi's grin grows and I narrow my eyes at him when I mouth, "Don't." He won't tell her about us. He can't, but he'll definitely use the situation to make me squirm.

"Nothin', Ma. Just a funny story. I'm sorry."

Relaxing against him, I run my hand over his chest, because yeah, I like touching him, but I'm not jerking him off when he's talking on the phone.

"I have to admit, I like hearing you laugh. I haven't said anything, but I've been a little worried about you, Levi. Something was different about you when you were home at Christmas. I'm pretty sure you thought you were playing it off well, but a mom knows. Every time I talk to you I hear it. I've been waiting for you to tell me what's going on."

At some point in her speech my hand stopped moving.

181

My heart maybe stops beating too, as I lie stiff beside Levi. His muscles are rigid as well.

Suddenly, my body gets antsy, and I try to get out of the bed again, needing space. Levi wraps his arm around me, holding me to him. I know I can get away if I really want, but maybe I don't want space as bad as I thought.

"I'm fine. Nothing to worry about," Levi tells her.

I try to tell him with my eyes that this is his chance to let her know about the changes in his life. It makes sense to start with Mrs. Baxter.

"You sure sound happy today," she says. "All that laughter pouring out of you. It reminded me of when you lived at home."

The world goes dark and I realize I'm closing my eyes, dropping my head, as though that will somehow shut out the sound of her voice. I don't know why I don't want to hear this conversation, but I don't.

"I am…I feel good. Better than I've felt in a long time, if I'm being honest. Better than I thought I could feel."

Each one of his words vibrates through me, echoing so I feel them in my chest. I know he's feeling good because he can pretend when he's with me, I get that, but it doesn't change the emotions swelling inside me. Emotions I want to evict the hell out of my chest.

"I need to tell you something," he says.

With that I jerk up, heart in my throat. My body's still close to his, my chest still touching him and my leg wrapped up with his, only now I'm propped on my elbow so I can look down at him. Is he going to tell her? Is he really going to admit he doesn't want to be a doctor?

From my new position, I can't hear Elaine anymore. She must tell him to continue because he does. "I'm seeing someone, Ma...and he's a guy."

Holy. Fucking. Shit. That was not what I expected him to say.

Frantically, I shake my head. He wouldn't tell her it's me. He can't. He knows I don't want Chris to know, but he doesn't know the extent of my reasons. Over the last few weeks I've thought about talking with him about Chris, but how do I tell him that his brother basically hates him? Hates him for reasons I now know are wrong? Levi would be crushed to hear it and he's already suffering under too much weight—

And wait... He said he's seeing someone? We're friends, friends who have sex on a regular basis. That's all we've ever discussed. Sure Brian's friend made a comment about boyfriends but it's not something Levi and I have ever talked about.

I don't know if he's ignoring my crazy headshaking or if he agrees with me, but he says, "No, not gay. I'm bisexual, though."

He's silent while I assume she's speaking.

"I didn't realize it until college. I never thought it was important enough to mention to you."

More silence from Levi. I'm holding my breath.

"No," he says finally. "I knew you wouldn't care."

My lungs burn so bad; I'm forcing myself to breathe. I knew she would be okay with it. Sometimes you just need to hear the affirmation, though.

"Thanks, Ma. I'm happy for me, too. Don't…don't say anything to Dad or Chris yet, okay?" His eyes hold me, and I wouldn't be able to look away from him even if I wanted to as he says, "I don't know what's going to happen yet, but I don't want to jinx it. I'm not sure if he's serious or not. I just know that I have fun with him. I want to be around him all the time."

My heart's beating so hard, he has to feel it in his chest. What he said is a lot to take in, a whole hell of a lot and I don't know what to say or think or feel, so instead I just watch him, feel his intense stare.

"No, I haven't told him how much I care about him. Let's not get carried away. I just think I need to take things slow with him. He probably wouldn't believe me if I told him I care about him. He's funny that way, so I'm just going to keep trying to show him until I wear him down. I mean, if you could tell the difference in me just from a phone call, you'd think he'd be able to see it, too."

And I do. I don't know how Levi is when he's at school, but Friday evening through Sunday evening, he shines with the qualities I've always admired about him. He's the guy who held the brightness of the whole fucking world inside him, sharing it with people. It killed me when I thought that light was starting to go out, and I know it'll be equally fucking devastating to me to lose it.

"What the hell, Mom?! No, he's not using me for sex!"

I have to bite my tongue not to laugh at that. I'm not even surprised those words came out of Elaine's mouth.

"I'm slightly uncomfortable that you said that. I need to

go bleach my brain, Ma. I'll call you later." Levi hangs up the phone and I lay my head on his chest. He rubs a hand over my short hair, and I soak it in, savor the feel of him, because that's a whole hell of a lot easier than speaking.

CHAPTER TWENTY-EIGHT

"You mad?" Levi asks after a long stretch of silence.

My thoughts roll around, wrestling each other in my head. "Mad? Nah. I can't be mad at that."

His voice drops an octave, his hold on me tighter. "Scared?"

It's then I realize maybe Levi knows me better than I thought. He sees more than most people, more than I show him. Because I *am* scared. "Yeah."

"Why?"

Why shouldn't I be is a better question. He's got so much going on inside his head and his heart right now—how can he sort through it all to know how he feels about me? And that's just the turmoil happening *inside* Levi. There's all the outside stuff to consider, too. The problems his family might have. The fact that I don't even know if I want a serious relationship.

I've seen what kind of fallout can happen with a serious relationship and I want nothing to do with it.

"Jesus, Toby. You say you love words so much but you can't seem to use them when it matters." He pushes away, sitting up with his back against the wall. I just let him be and don't touch him as he continues, "It's not like I said I want to get married, adopt babies and live the American Dream with you. I'm saying I like hanging out. You make me feel good. I care about you and I want to keep doing this and feel like we're on the same fucking page, man. I'm always chasing after you when I've never chased anyone in my life."

Of course, it has to come back to that. "Oh for fuck's sake. Sorry to put a dent in the great Levi Baxter's ego." He flinches and immediately the angry fire inside me is doused and replaced by guilt. "Shit. I didn't mean that." Bowing my head, I close my eyes. Try to find my words. "We're on the same page. I don't know why this is so hard for me."

The bed dips and my pulse automatically speeds up, my skin eager for the touch I know he's going to give me. "It's hard because you don't let anyone in, no one except my brother. It's hard because you don't want to be left. It's hard because it matters."

Yes, yes, and yes. He hit the nail on the head with all of those things. "Maybe." I grin.

Levi's finger hooks beneath my chin. When he tilts my head up, I open my eyes and the way our gazes connect so fast and so completely, I feel like we're seeing each other as we truly are. "See? That wasn't so hard was it?" Levi pushes onto his knees, crawls over me and straddles my lap. My dick grows, hardens as it stands at attention, the velvet skin of his length against mine. "What are you doing for spring break?"

"Spring break? You're naked on my lap and want to talk about something weeks away? I can't think beyond my next orgasm right now."

He chuckles, winks and damned if I'm not honored that it's me who gets to see this side of him. Me who knows both the old Levi and the new Levi and how they blend together.

"Maybe that's my plan." He leans forward, nips my neck with his teeth and then kisses the tender skin.

"Chris..." I gasp out, my thoughts trying to become clear.

"That's my brother, not me." He bites again and I buck before he kisses the same spot for the second time.

"No shit. Not a chance I'm mixing the two of you up... He's taking Gemma home again. I'm supposed to go back, too. He wants to do this concert thing in Portland."

"Oh..." One more soft kiss that goes straight to my balls, before he pulls away. "I was hoping you were staying. I'm supposed to go back, but I want to skip out. I don't feel like lying. I gotta lie when I go there."

But he doesn't. He really fucking doesn't. "Just tell them. I'll...I'll go with you if you want. Not that I can do anything, but I'll be there."

He smiles like I gave him the answer to everything he's ever wanted, when all I did was offer to sit next to him while he's honest to his parents.

"Thank you. I can't take you up on that. You know I can't quit, Tobias. Just thinking about it overwhelms me with so much fucking stress I want to explode. But I'm thankful you'd offer." There's this quiet honesty in Levi sometimes that I never noticed before the past couple months. When he says something's important to him, he means it. He's not the guy who says shit just to say it.

And then, all I can think about is how it would feel to spend the week here with him compared to what it would be like going home.

Home where I spend time with my dad and become just like him—the two loneliest men in the world living side by side.

Home where I'd end up lying to Chris and hearing him talk shit about Levi when he doesn't deserve it. Not this Levi.

"Xavier won't be here," I say, not sure why.

"I know."

His hair tickles my forehead when he leans closer. My head bows and I look down at his long erection and the pearl of liquid at the tip of his thick rod. I want this. Want him. Just to chill, and enjoy my time with him.

If I bail on going home, though, Chris won't understand. Hell, I don't understand—it's not the kind of thing I've ever done before. We made plans. I'm always there for Chris the same way he's always been there for me. But the thought of staying here with Levi fills up the hollow space inside me. Thinking about going home only makes the space bigger.

"I'll stay."

"Fuck yesss…Oh yeah…" Levi says when I wrap my hand around our dicks.

As I stroke us together, my thumb rubbing around his head, my head, smearing our pre-come together, Levi thrusts into my hand, riding my lap. It's not long before I feel the tingle in my sac, before my balls draw up tight and then I groan, coming all over us. Levi pumps into my hand one more time before he's joining me, our fluid running down my fingers and our stomachs.

"I'm dying. That felt so damn good." He rolls off me and onto the bed. I go down beside him. The room is warm, but it's not enough to make me ease my sweat-slicked body away from his.

After a few minutes, he asks, "Why doesn't Chris ever ask me to do stuff with him? Like the concert? I mean, I get why he wouldn't when we were kids—we were pretty different—but things have changed now. "

I know now how things have changed for Levi. But they're not different for Chris, and I don't have the heart to tell Levi. If I add Chris's shit to the pile, it won't do any of us any good. Chris's anger at Levi in the past didn't bother me, but now it hurts like hell because I know how much it would devastate Levi.

I've started to feel as solid with Levi as I do with Chris. I feel like he sees my true colors with his artist's eyes. Worrying about Chris is kind of like splashing paint thinner on what Levi and I are building together—it's eating away at my colors. "I don't know," I finally respond.

"Liar," he whispers, and then, "I wish I could take some of it back."

"Like what?"

He pauses a minute as though he's thinking. "Just how I acted. How I thought. I know some of the shit I did was obnoxious. Part of it was me being an asshole, me thinking that I could do anything but it was more than that, too. I think since I thought I *had* to be so perfect, I tried too hard to play the golden boy role, ya know? Had to talk shit to feel better about myself and had to have girls so I could feel wanted. Pretty shitty, right?"

There's bone deep sadness to his voice that splinters my insides. I can see what he's saying. See how Levi wasn't always as confident as we thought. See how he just tried to be who everyone thought he was, or who everyone thought he should be. "There's nothing we can do about the past." Him or me.

"Do you remember that girl Chris hooked me up with that one time? Bridget or something like that."

Wait. "What?" I look at him.

"Bridget. She was that girl who liked me. She told Chris and he brought her around so she could get to know me."

Wow. This puts a whole new spin on things. It also helps make sense of Levi's odd thanks way back then. "That's not what happened. If she told you that she lied. She made Chris think she liked him. He thought they were dating, and the next thing he knew, you were taking her out."

Levi's eyes go wide as he sits up. "Are you serious?"

"Yeah." And I can't help but wonder if there were more misunderstandings with Levi in the past. Not that I think he was perfect, because I don't, but things aren't always what they seem.

"Holy shit." He runs a hand though his hair. "Chris must have wanted to kill me." He takes a deep breath, closes his eyes, the sadness making his body look heavier. Levi lies back down beside me. "Why didn't he say anything?"

"I don't know." I do know that I want to comfort him though. Rolling over, I kiss him before pulling him close.

With my arm wrapped around him and my face in his neck, I hold Levi until he goes to sleep.

CHAPTER TWENTY-NINE

We're both busy as hell the next couple weeks. When he comes on the weekend we spend most of our time doing homework. I watch him sometimes, having no fucking clue how he does all the shit he does. The fact that he's smart as hell becomes even more obvious as I watch him work through microbiology, immunology, and other "ology's" that I didn't know existed.

He's a perfectionist—I've always known this about him—but the longer we spend time together, the more I see it in everything he does. The more I understand that's why this whole thing is so hard for him.

He will make a damn good doctor if he goes through with it. He's kind enough and he has the big brain for it. His heart is for sure big enough, but to do the job and be happy, his heart has to be *in* the idea of being a doctor, too.

It's a Tuesday the week after I told him I'd stay for spring break. I'm on my fifteen at work, sitting in the little-ass break room when I pull out my phone. **Hey…what's up? How's your day?**

Levi's reply comes almost instantly. **Shitty day. Really busy. Sorry I didn't text…but then, maybe that's a good thing. This is the first time you've messaged me first.**

Which can't really be true, can it? How can I not have messaged Levi first? **Shut up.**

I'm serious.

Honestly, I know he must be serious. I don't get it. Why do I have this block inside me for shit like that? Why don't I just pick up the phone because I want to talk to him and text or call? Because I do. I want to talk to him all the time. **Sorry.**

Don't be. Just do it more often now, yeah? Oh! I have a plan. For every time you text me first, I'll let you suck my dick first the next time we see each other.

I laugh so hard, my cheeks start to hurt. **Fuck you. Shouldn't it be the other way around?**

Nah, you love sucking dick, T. You want me in your mouth.

And he's right, I really do. **Deal.**

That's what I thought. You're the best. I gotta go but, did you tell Chris yet? I talked to Mom last night and she said something about you and Chris for spring break.

Fuck. The laughter in my gut turns into something else entirely. Dread and guilt, because I'm putting this off for no reason. We're supposed to head home next week, and Chris still doesn't know I won't be there. **It's on my list. Gotta go too. See you this weekend.**

There's a delay, a long one, before Levi replies. **See ya.**

***

194

It's strange having people depend on you. Depend might not be the right word, I guess, but the concept has never really come up for me before.

Up until now the only people I've been close to are Chris and my dad. And with my dad's issues, that always meant Chris was the guy I relied on, the guy I wanted to hang with. He's always been my boy.

Now Levi's become such a big part of my life, I'm having to think harder about how my actions affect people. It would hurt Chris if I ditched him for his brother. He already thinks everyone chooses Levi over him. How can I be that guy to Chris?

My brain keeps telling me I have to choose between them. I don't want to. I like things easy and all this heart-to-brain back and forth makes me want to just say *fuck it* and walk away from it all.

But I don't.

My need to spend time with Levi is huge and consuming and it surprises the hell out of me every day. The need for someone like him in my life was buried deep, a pebble of a desire that's snowballed until it's gotten so big, I'm not sure there's room for anything else. It's uncomfortable and scary and something I would ordinarily hate, but apparently I like the feeling. Because I don't ever want to change it.

So two days before I'm supposed to go to Oregon, I call Chris.

"Hey, bro, what's up?" he says before, "Hold on, baby. It's Toby."

"Hi, Toby!" Gemma shouts in the background.

My guilt takes on massive proportions. Canceling this late makes me a really big asshole.

"Tell her I say hi…and I have some bad news. I'm not going to be able to make it up to Coburn for spring break. Things are crazy at work and I need to pick up some extra shifts." Apparently being an asshole isn't my only shitty quality. I'm a liar, too.

"What? No way, man. That sucks. You can't get out of it? We didn't get to do much over Christmas."

Weighing my words, I try to think of the best way to reply to make me even a little bit less of a lying asshole. "I wish there was a way I could do both. I miss your dumb ass, but I made a commitment, and it's really important." All true.

Chris sighs. "Damn… I wish I would have known sooner. We almost went to Gem's, but you and I had plans and I didn't want to skip out on you."

Fuck. What the hell am I doing? I squeeze my eyes closed. I hadn't thought about the possibility he could have made other plans if it weren't for me.

That's the thing about Chris. He's the guy who would sacrifice getting to know his girlfriend's family if he thought it was best for me and here I am, fucking things up for a piece of his brother's ass.

But that's not really what this is about. Levi's more than that…

"I'm sorry, man. I feel like shit. Maybe there's something I can do—"

"Nah, I get it. If you have to work, you have to work. It sucks, but that's the way it is."

That was nice of him, pushing the knife in further by trying to be a good guy. "I'll make it up to you, Chris." Because I really don't know what I would do without him.

"It's cool. I got you. We're good. I'm gonna go, though. I was just about to kiss my girlfriend senseless when you called—ouch! Shit. No hitting, Gem!"

I can't help but laugh at their games and see the same kind of conversation going down between Levi and I.

CHAPTER
THIRTY

"You're nervous, aren't you?" Levi nudges my arm as
we walk down the street. The sun's high and bright enough to
burn my eyes, but the air's still cool. Spring is teasing us, but
hasn't really blessed us with her presence yet.

He's wearing my San Francisco State University hoodie.
We fought over it this morning. I don't know why he loves
the damn thing so much, but he's always jacking it from me.
A few weeks ago he took it back to Palo Alto with him when
he left on Sunday, so I ended up going out and buying the
plain black hoodie that I'm now stuck wearing.

"No. Why would I be nervous?" But I am, and both Levi
and I know it. It's a good question for me to ask, though. Just
because I feel something doesn't mean I understand it. Does
anyone truly understand their feelings? Or do we all like to
pretend we have the answers, when half the time we're all just
floating along and hoping for the best.

"Because this is pretty close to legit boyfriend stuff.
We're not just fucking like rabbits and hiding out in your
apartment. We're going to lunch with your friend and her

boyfriend. It's like a double date."

Rolling my eyes at him, I say, "It's not a double date."

"Is too."

"Is not."

"Is too."

"Dude, I'm going to kick your ass if you don't stop trying to argue with me all the time!" Playfully, I push him. Levi stumbles, laughing, but grabs onto my arm to steady himself. It's a reflex for me, reaching down and locking our fingers together. It's so fairytale-cheesy in so many ways. Frolicking down the street holding a dude's hand was never something I really saw myself doing, but I like the feel of Levi's hand in mine. His skin feels rougher—there's a callous from his pencil on his finger because he's been drawing so much.

"You didn't argue about the boyfriend stuff." He squeezes my hand. No, I didn't, and I'm not sure how I feel about that. "You're into me, Tobias Jackson. Not just the fantasy Levi. You like *me*. I got past your defenses, didn't I?" When I don't answer, he adds, "It's okay. I like you, too. You've known that for a while, though. I've never had a boyfriend before. I think I like it."

It's just like Levi to run with this, for him to decide we're now boyfriends and that's the way it is. It's kind of a surprise how much I love that about him.

Returning his brief squeeze from earlier, I reply, "Well who wouldn't? It's me." Translation: I like you too, but I'm too weak to really say it.

"Wow…you didn't trip or anything when you said that.

You're not clumsy around me anymore. I miss it." Levi lets go of my hand before wrapping his arm around my neck, keeping us close. "Or maybe I don't… I like that you're comfortable around me. Another sign I'm not fantasy Levi anymore. I'm real."

I look over at him as we make our way down the sidewalk. He nods and I kiss his cheek. I pay attention to where we're going so I really don't trip. No one looks twice at us. I needed that when I came to San Francisco. Needed not to be different. Not the only black kid or the only queer kid. We're just Toby and Levi, and damned if I don't like the sound of our names together.

"That chick in front of us is smiling like someone just handed her a million dollars. Let me guess, that's Cherise?" Levi winks, making my stomach roll. He still does that shit to me, makes me crazy with need, the bastard.

"Yep, that's her. Beware. She's great, but she's…eager. She's wanted to meet you for a while."

Levi shakes his head and rolls his eyes as though I'm being ridiculous. "Please. I know how to handle women. It's a specialty of mine."

"Better not be anymore."

"Nah, not like that. I have no interest in handling anyone except the guy who just admitted he's my boyfriend." And then he pulls away. "Hey! I'm Levi. You must be Cherise. It's so great to finally meet you."

Levi gives her a smile and I swear to God she swoons. Bastard. I'm going to kick his ass for that later.

***

"Toby was fucking adorable when I first met him. He was this skinny little kid, all bones and long limbs, following my brother around. But you could tell he had so much more going on inside. He'd try to hide it, being all tough guy and 'I don't need anyone'. There was this one time..."

I drop my head back and look at the ceiling as Levi tells the third embarrassing Toby memory from our past. Both Brian and Cherise are paying rapt attention, hanging onto every word because this is fucking Levi and that's what people do when it comes to him. He's charming and funny, everyone sees it, but I'm wishing he would shut the hell up on memories of young Toby.

"So it wasn't until this past Christmas break that you noticed Levi—like in a way that was more than just friends?" Brian asks me when Levi's done recounting his latest memory. Brian's a cool guy, totally comfortable in any situation. I dig that about him.

"I didn't know he was bisexual until then. It surprised the hell out of me," I admit.

"So?" Levi says. "That doesn't mean *I* didn't notice *you.*"

Well *this* is an interesting development. "Go on," I encourage. "I approve of this story. Not the others, though."

Everyone at the table laughs.

"It's strange," Levi says, "because even though I was thirteen when Toby came into our lives, it's almost like he was always there. He was like my kid brother in a lot of ways, which is weird to think about now, but it's true. He and Chris were attached at the hip." Levi reaches over, grabs a French fry off my plate and eats it before continuing. "Once I left for college and had more experience—and then when he went away and came home for breaks—I noticed him. The summer after his freshman year was the first time. He was swimming at our house and I noticed he'd grown a whole hell of a lot since he left for school." He smiles at me. "It's probably safer I stop there."

Everyone laughs again and Levi's eating it up. Me? I'm wanting him to finish that story. I can't believe he never told me.

After lunch, an hour or so later, we're walking back to my apartment when I ask, "How about you finish that story now? You were holding out on me!"

He wrinkles his nose. "No thank you. I'm surprised you've held out for this long before asking."

"No thank you? No thank you? How can you say that? Dude, I wanted you and now I find out you noticed me earlier, too?"

Levi crosses his arms playfully. "A man has to have some secrets."

"Not this one."

We're at the apartment now, and when we stop at the entrance he hooks a finger into one of the belt loops on my jeans. "I could probably be persuaded…"

Okay, so this might not be so bad. I can handle persuading him if it means I get off and get the information I want. "How do you mean?"

He leans in, his mouth close to my ear, his breath hot on my skin. "Fuck me hard enough and I'm putty in your hands, Tobias. We'll pretend that's what it takes, when we both know that with or without the lay, I'm already yours. I'm not sure there's a damn thing I wouldn't do for you."

My chest swells like someone's pumping it up, pushing a lever over and over to inflate it, and there's nothing I can do to stop it. I feel Levi there, inside me, changing me, making all these emotions come alive that I never thought would be there.

"But there's a catch... To find out, you still have to fuck me. And to fuck me, you have to catch me." And then he's gone, running up the stairs to my apartment and I'm rushing after him, wanting my prize.

CHAPTER THIRTY-ONE

The next few days are strange and wonderful. Levi's in my bed every night and every morning. We cook meals together. He's home when I go to work and there when I get home. He'll be sitting at the table drawing, or in my bed waiting and suddenly...I get it. Get how having something like this can be addicting. How it can change your world in both scary and incredible ways.

And I've also seen how losing it can change you. I think that's what happened to my dad, but now I'm seeing the flip side. I'm understanding the part of love that doesn't tear you apart.

It's halfway through spring break when I get home from work around four. I'm tired as hell. Today was an early shift. I actually did pick up more hours over break because I can always use the money. It also eases some of the guilt where Chris is concerned. The reason I stayed in San Francisco wasn't a total lie.

The second I walk in the door, Levi says, "I have a surprise for you. Let's go take a shower and I'll tell you while we're in there."

"Why do I have to be in the shower with you for you to tell me?"

"Do you really need a reason to be in the shower with me?" he tosses back.

"Good point. Let's go."

We're naked and standing under the spray of my noisy-ass, incredibly small shower, my dick growing because yeah, we're naked and wet and my dick always likes the idea of getting off, when Levi says, "We're going out."

That definitely wasn't what I expected him to say. "We already had social time this week when we went to lunch with Cherise and Brian. Can't we stay home? Spend the rest of the day in this shower instead?" I reach for him, wrap my hand around his hardening length and stroke.

Levi hisses. "Well, you're welcome to make me come first, but we're still going out. I owe you a play, since you didn't go back home."

As I look him in the eyes, my hand pauses, stops pumping on his hot, thick erection. "We're going to the theater?" My heart's slam-dancing against my chest.

"Yeah…it's not the same play. I don't know if you've seen it or if you'll like it, but even if it sucks, I figured I'd get points for trying." He laughs but I can't bring myself to return his laughter. It's such a small thing in so many ways, but this is the second time Levi has tried to give me something I love. The second time he's made the offer to see a play with me because he knows I'd enjoy it, even though he's not totally sure he will.

Sometimes it's the smallest sacrifices, the smallest ways you try to make someone happy that mean the most. "You don't need any more points than you already have. You have more points than anyone in my life, ever."

Levi tries. My dad has never tried. My mom just walked away. Hell, I don't try, not with most people, but he makes me want to.

The water starts to turn cold, but neither of us makes the move to get out.

"You're good at words when you use them. I wish you did it more," Levi says softly.

"I know… I'm trying." And I am.

He cups my face, brushes a thumb across my cheek. We're shivering now, his teeth clattering in the cold water. His wet, brown hair hangs in his face. I like it like that. His pale skin will have a blue tint to it soon if we don't get out.

"If you kiss me, I'll tell you what we're seeing," he finally says.

"You're always trying to bribe me. You don't have to." Our lips are cold against each other's. He trembles and I tremble but it's worth my body freezing to have my tongue in his mouth, to taste him and eat his moans and feed him my own.

When we pull apart we're both panting and I'm really wanting him to get on his knees for me, or turn around and give himself to me—mouth or ass, I wouldn't care which way, but there's also excitement skittering through my veins, making my heart pump harder and faster. "So, what are we seeing?"

"*The Importance of Being Earnest.* Is that okay?"

"It's perfect." Anything would be.

***

After our shower we get dressed and then Uber it to a restaurant for dinner. We eat at a fresh seafood place. Levi orders a fucking lobster, but I go with fish and chips. I pay for dinner, even though Levi argues with me about it; but he bought the tickets, he planned this whole night, I'm not going to let him pay for dinner on top of it.

Maybe that's shitty dating etiquette, but it's how I feel. I don't have a lot of experience with this stuff. When I moved here, I became a slut because I wanted sex and experience and freedom. Somehow my life has been flipped upside down and I'm dating Levi. I need to admit it—I'm dating Levi Baxter. He's taking me out tonight.

We finish dinner and walk to the theater from there.

"So what's this play about?" he asks when we're almost there.

"You don't know?"

He looks sheepish when he replies, "Yeah, I totally know. Just checking to make sure you do."

Funny guy. So I tell him about the two friends, Jack and Algernon who make up fake personas to get the women they want to marry them, because they'll only marry an "earnest" man. He listens and seems interested, and when we get seated in the auditorium, Levi's full attention is on the stage. He laughs when he's supposed to, and leans forward to pay attention. He's passionate about it, in a way I didn't expect. It's not until the play is over that I realize I watched him more than the performance, and I've never enjoyed what I see more than I enjoy seeing Levi Baxter.

CHAPTER THIRTY-TWO

The second we get inside my apartment, my mouth covers Levi's. I want to crawl inside him, live there, taste and know and memorize every millimeter of his skin. Everything inside him. I want our bodies to know each other's in every way because everything about him feels so fucking good. Because seeing him happy makes me feel happy, too. I think maybe Levi spent his whole life not really believing he was truly happy until recently. Now his happiness is true and honest and beautiful.

I want to fuck his brains out, but I want to love him slowly, too. So we're a combination of urgency and easy exploration as we rip at each other's shirts, teeth clacking as we kiss, our hands slowing to rub and touch skin again and again.

Our shirts and shoes are gone in the living room. We're unbuttoning pants in the hallway. He kisses my neck, grabs my crotch, plucks my nipple, before saying, "I'll be right back. Be naked when I get there."

Levi makes his way into the bathroom, and I go into the

bedroom, kicking out of my slacks and underwear as I go. My usual doubts try to sneak into my consciousness—it's ironic that every time I go out of my mind for Levi like this I've still got shit hovering in my periphery. *This won't last forever. He won't be able to work through all the shit in his life, and he'll leave you. You aren't cut out for relationships.*

I fall back onto my bed, stroke my erection and just try to concentrate on how he makes me feel and seeing him smile and being inside him.

Feels like both an eternity and no time at all before Levi comes out, naked and hard. He sets his clothes on the dresser before walking toward me. "I love your skin." Levi kneels on the bed, leans over and kisses my stomach.

"I used to hate it," I admit.

"What?" He pulls back, but I shake my head and he starts kissing my chest.

"That's a lie, I guess. I didn't hate it. I just wished I wasn't different from everyone I knew. Gay guy, black guy…"

"My guy," he says. "And it's sexy as hell, the soft brown. I like to see us together. It's fucking hot."

And it is, his pale skin against mine. It's beautiful. "Come here," I tell him and Levi comes. His body runs the length of mine, his weight on me like it belongs there. Our mouths fuse, our tongues fight and wrestle as we thrust against each other.

The slow burn starts in my balls, our skin is dewy with sweat but we just keep kissing. Rolling over, I give Levi my weight now, thrust against his hot length as his hands clutch my ass. "You know you can have me, too. Anytime. I like to bottom, as well. I know you said—"

"I want you. I'll have you," he interrupts.

"Good." I know he said in the beginning that when he's with a guy, he likes to be fucked, but I want him to know I go both ways. I *want* it both ways from time to time.

"Next time. Just like you inside me so fucking much," he says and then we're kissing again and my head is threatening to explode just from hearing him say that.

Levi kisses and licks my throat and Adam's apple as I reach over for the lube and condoms. He spreads his legs and I kneel between them, ripping open the condom and covering my sensitive erection. "Hold your legs back for me."

It's fucking gorgeous to see him like this, all laid bare and open for me. Squirting lube in my hand I wet his hole, my erection, and then play with him a little more. Pushing a finger inside, I tease him, finger him, just reveling in the way he feels from the inside.

"Let's do this," Levi tells me after a minute. "Give it to me." Leaning forward, I take his mouth. My tongue pushes inside at the same moment I breach his body, feel all the tight heat around me.

"You feel so good," I tell him.

Levi answers with a strangled-out, "Then show me."

So I do, pulling out and thrusting back home over and over. The bed hits the wall. My balls beg to empty. He grunts and moans and grabs my ass. It's harder than it usually is, but slower, too. More intimate as our eyes hold each other's and my hand knots in his hair.

He just called me his and, even though I didn't set out to

do it, now I'm claiming him.

I can tell when he's close because he starts jerking himself off. The second he erupts, his body tightening around me, I let loose, giving him my orgasm before collapsing on top of his sticky body.

He sucks in a deep breath, so I roll off him without going far. We're still touching, still glued together with sweat and come. Our breathing alternates: him in, me out, him out, me in, and as crazy as it sounds, I find a strange comfort in that. It's as though we're working together, making a rhythm between the two of us.

"We can go to the theater every damned night if you do me like that afterward." Leaning over, he kisses my forehead. "Your hair's growing out a little. I like it."

Closing my eyes, I savor the feel of his hand rubbing my head. "That feels awesome. I might have to keep it like this." And then his previous comment comes back to me. "Thanks for tonight. We should do something you like tomorrow."

"I like this."

As much as I enjoy hearing that, as much as it makes me feel invincible, I answer honestly. "You have to like more than just this, though. You should love what you do. You shouldn't plan your life around doing shit that makes everyone else happy."

Levi sighs. This probably wasn't the best time to go there, but it's done now. I wouldn't take it back if I could.

"Okay, so I'll keep doing what I'm doing because I don't know what else to do. Or because I've sacrificed five years of my life for it already. Five fucking years, Tobias. Or because I've worked my ass off. Or because my family spent an incredible amount of money on my college and med school. Most people don't love what they do. People make decisions and then they follow through with them. That's what life is."

I picture my dad when he says that. See him going through the motions every damn day and not enjoying any of it. He doesn't try to make any changes, just keeps going on the same path he set out on years ago. "Fuck that."

"Can we not do this? I just blew my load and I'd much rather pass the hell out than argue with you. Let's just enjoy the night."

But I can't do that. Maybe he doesn't get how or why I'm sure of it, but he can't live that kind of life. Not Levi. He can't be okay with just going through the motions. What hope do the rest of us have if someone like Levi can't do what makes him happy?

"My dad doesn't talk to me," I tell him. "He doesn't know how. He let out a relieved breath when I told him I wasn't coming home for spring break."

Levi shakes his head. "That can't be true. He wouldn't—"

"He did. Do I think he doesn't love me? No…not really, but do I think he's so fucking unhappy with his life that he'd rather be alone? Yes. Do I think he'd rather soak in memories than make sure he knows his son? Yes."

He's still petting my head, his voice low as he says, "That's not me. I'm sorry about your dad, but that's not me. My job will be one aspect of my life. That's it. I have no problem living my life. Being friends with people. Telling people how I feel. Making a responsible decision about my career, hell, planning to save lives is hardly the same thing as what your dad has been going through with his life."

I'm arguing with myself because I partly feel like he's right. Most people aren't happy with their careers. But then... "You deserve to be happy. You deserve to have what you want."

Levi sighs. "What am I going to do with you?" he asks. The sincerity in his husky voice draws my gaze to his.

Don't leave. Just don't fucking walk away.

"Everyone deserves to be happy. I'm trying to get there. I feel closer to that place than I did six months ago. When I'm in this bed, I'm happy. When I'm with you."

Whether that's true or not, it can't be everything.

CHAPTER THIRTY-THREE

We spend the morning at an art supply store, the heavy tone of last night's conversation hanging in the air around us, but not managing to weigh down our time together completely. Neither of us are dumb guys. Fear of failing or not, Levi has to know the truth about what he's doing. He has to know that this is a decision he needs to make for himself, even if he *does* eventually decide to continue on this path.

It's similar to how I know I allow my personal fears to come between us. How I don't give myself to Levi as openly as he's offering himself to me. How I want to believe his words, want to feel that they're Levi's truth, and yet I'm not sure I'm worthy of them at the same time.

We make a stop by the library on the way home and then we're back in the apartment I share with Xavier. We're in my room, me lying on the bed, back against the wall and my book in my hand. Levi sits on the bed's edge, an easel in front of him, charcoal pencil sketching out my bedroom of all things.

He doesn't move, doesn't flinch when I run a finger down his spine, and tease the edge of his underwear, the only thing he has on. "You're lost."

"Just drawing," he says. "And thinking. Did you really struggle with being the only black kid in town? Did people give you shit?" He doesn't turn around and I know it's because he's trying to make it easier for me to talk about this stuff.

I've been thinking about Levi's truth, but I haven't been real about my own. About the fact that even though I kept telling myself it was a necessity, I didn't keep my distance from him. My heart beats his name. There was no way I could be with Levi Baxter and not fall in love with him. Maybe I always have been in one way or another, but this little thing— him giving me his back, the way he creates a space that makes me feel safe enough to share shit I never share—makes me realize he's already totally made his way inside my heart.

"No…not really," I answer him. "They didn't give me shit, but… No one wants to be different, Levi. Especially when you're a kid. When you're trying to find your place in the world. And home—where you're supposed to feel the most comfortable—is full of people who don't look like you, it's tough sometimes. I stood out when I never wanted to stand out. Even when people treated me just like they did everyone else, I didn't feel white enough. Add being gay on top of that, and yeah, living in Coburn made me feel like I was naked all the fucking time."

He turns toward me at that, lying on his stomach and leaning on his elbows. "Chris?"

"Yeah…he helped. I was always just Toby to him. It was two days after my mom left that he came up to me at recess and started talking to me. Maybe I clung to him because he just kept talking day after day when I needed someone most, but he was my boy. Always. Chris was there for me without really trying. He's the first person I told I'm gay and he just shrugged, said cool and then made a comment about there being more girls for him. I needed that. He never once acted weird about it. " And then I came here and I felt like I had to start over. I was the gay kid at home who never felt white enough. When I came here I was the gay kid with zero experience who didn't always feel black enough.

"You have me hating my brother." But then he winks and smiles. "I'm kidding. I'm glad you had him. He's a good guy...Chris. I feel pretty fucking lucky that he's my brother. I wish we were closer."

I wish they were, too.

"I like it when you talk to me."

I like talking to him as well. It's a strange sensation, this feeling that I'm adjusting to as it settles in my chest.

Before I reply, the shrill ring of his cell makes my heart thud. Levi laughs. "It scared you. Your eyes almost popped out. Don't worry, I'll save you."

Shaking my head at him, I watch as he reaches for his phone. I'm pretty sure I left mine in the living room when we got home a few hours ago.

"It's Chris," he says, frowning. Chris doesn't call Levi. It's just not something he does.

Levi answers with, "What's wrong?" instead of hello. I push to the edge of the bed, sit there watching him. There's a pause while Levi listens. The hand holding the phone starts to tremble. "Is he okay?" Levi looks at me, his eyes going soft around the edges, sadness playing over his features.

"Absolutely. I'll take care of it. Right now. What's the address?" Levi asks. Address? Whose address would he need? Unless it's somewhere he has to go as soon as he gets back home.

"No shit, Chris. I'm not a fucking idiot. I'll take care of him." There's a struggle Levi's fighting. I see it in all of his features, the way he glances down. When his head slowly tilts until he's looking at me, he's all sadness, like he's made of it. I'm made up of fear. Something's wrong and I need to know what.

Levi ends the call, tosses his phone to the bed, and then runs a hand through his hair. The truth is hidden inside me. It has to be. Levi showed it to me in the way he looked at me, the way he won't look at me now. This is about me...but I don't want to believe it. "Is it your dad? Did something happen?" I ask him.

"No, baby," he replies. It's the first time he's called me that, and now's the wrong time to think about it or care about it, but it's his word choice I choose to focus on. It's a whole hell of a lot easier than thinking of anything else. *Baby.* It's not something I ever would have thought I'd want to be called, but hearing Levi say it is like cotton candy, an orgasm, and winning the lottery all in one.

"Just tell me. I need you to fucking tell me." I'm rocking, my hands wringing together uncontrollably.

He slides off the bed and kneels between my legs. "Your dad got into a car accident. He's at the hospital now, in the ICU. I'm sorry." Levi wraps his arms around me, his soft fingers dancing across the skin of my back.

It's him touching me that I want to feel. Levi's skin on

mine. His arms around me. My lips on his, my dick inside him, not this other stuff. Not the ache that's spreading through my gut, breaking into my chest and trying to crack it open. Not my heart crumbling into dust.

He's my dad. I can't lose him.

"He'll be okay. My dad's making sure of it. We need to get you home. Pack some shit, and we'll get you home to see him." Levi's knee pops when he stands up and reaches for his clothes.

Still I don't move. I can't. My bones are set in stone, my mind the only thing capable of moving. *I'm going to lose him. I'm going to lose him. I'm going to lose him.*

"Hey." Levi's hand tightens on the back of my neck. I didn't realize he'd even approached to touch me. "He's going to be okay, Tobias. I promise you, okay? He's going to be fine."

But he can't make a promise like that and both of us know it.

"You sit right there. I'll pack everything up for you. We'll be out of here in no time. You're going to have to get dressed, though." He winks at me. I appreciate the effort, but I can't smile at him in return.

When I stand, Levi is there again. He pulls me into another hug, and I sag against him, let him hold me up. I bury my face into his neck, his left arm under my right one, his hand on my back. Closing my eyes, I imagine his hair in his face and it's almost enough to make me smile.

"Why did Chris call you?" I ask when I pull away.

Levi's features tighten, and then just like that, they're

back to normal. It happened so quickly, I'm not sure I really saw it.

"Your phone's in the other room. Maybe it's on vibrate or something. When he couldn't get ahold of you, he had no choice except to call me and ask me to drive here from Palo Alto to let you know. Believe me, he didn't want to. He doesn't trust me with coming here to get you and making sure you get home okay. I was just the only option he had."

CHAPTER THIRTY-FOUR

Unfortunately, we couldn't get a flight out right away. It's the middle of the night when we leave which gets us to Portland early the next morning. Levi hasn't touched me since we got here. They air-lifted my dad here after the accident. Levi's no-touching thing is for me. Usually I'd appreciate his efforts, but right now I want him to touch me, I want the comfort only he can give. If I told him, he'd offer it freely.

On the way here, I'd made sure to call Chris so he knew I was coming. I also had to make the call down South to talk to my grandma, who can't make it. She would be here for Dad if she could, it's killing her not to, but she recently had back surgery.

We arrive in the ICU waiting room, and immediately see Chris. He shoves to his feet. Gemma's asleep in a chair, and Elaine gives me a sad smile. There's no friends from work, or anyone else here for my dad. Just Levi's family.

Chris's eyes dart to Levi, and I see confusion there. What? Did he think Levi would just tell me my dad's unconscious in the ICU and then send me on my way? That's not how Levi rolls. But then, Chris doesn't know that, does he? In Chris's eyes, Levi's the same guy who's always driven him up a fucking wall.

"Hey, buddy. How you doing?" Chris wraps his arms around me and pulls me into a hug. His support is important to me. I lean into him, let him hold me up. He's the only one who tried to hold me up until recently.

"Okay, I guess," I say into his neck. There's nothing like the comfort of a best friend. It doesn't ever go away, not with a friendship as strong as ours. "I'm scared."

"I know. Come on. I'll take you to see him." Since Chris's dad works here, no one argues with Chris coming back with me. He leads me around the busy nurses' station, through the ICU doors, and then past another quieter nurses' station.

Ridiculously, my first thought is Levi might work here one day. He might be a doctor trying to help someone's loved one survive...and I'd trust him with that. He has a big heart and he's smart. He'd be good at this. But would he *love* this?

"He's in bed three, right over here." Chris nods toward a room, and I follow him over. As soon as I step inside, my legs almost give out. I have to grab onto the wall so I don't hit the floor.

His dark skin is pale, almost unreal-looking. There's a breathing tube in his throat and IV's hooked up to him. Machines beep and hiss and pump air into him. Keep him alive.

My dad. The only parent I have left. The one who stayed. I'm still standing in the doorway because if I don't step all the way inside, maybe this isn't real.

"He's in a medically induced coma for now. They said if things stay stable enough, they'll hopefully be able to try and pull him out of it in a few days."

"Okay." It's a nothing reply. There's no feeling or meaning behind it, but it's the best I have right now.

"We took care of as much as we could from our end. You're going to have to give them some of his information."

"Okay," I reply again, watching the machines as they breathe for him and medicate him and do whatever else they're doing.

"Go sit with him, T. It's okay."

My brain doesn't seem to be working. My body moves, but it's robotic, almost like something else is controlling me. I walk over and sit in the chair. Chris takes the one beside me and we sit in silence for close to an hour, watching my dad lay there.

It's Chris's scratchy voice that breaks the silence. "Do you want to be alone with him?"

No. "Yeah. Thanks, man."

"I'm going to take Mom and Gemma home so they can get some rest, grab some food and then I'll be back, okay?"

"No." I shake my head. "You've been here all night and day. You go get some sleep, too. I'll be fine. I'll call you later."

"No, I can't do that. I'm not sure if Mom or Gemma should be driving, though. They're exhausted. I'll see if Levi can take them and I'll stay here with you. I'll be in the waiting room until you're ready."

My heartbeat picks up at the mention of Levi's name. I'd walked away from him in the waiting area without a word. I've been sitting here for an hour and didn't even take the time to thank him for coming with me. For keeping me sane. He's been up all night and day as well.

"Yeah, I'm sure he'll do that." The words that come out of my mouth are at war with those inside me. The ones saying, "No, I need Levi. Need his strength."

I don't want Levi to go with them. I want him to stay with me.

Chris squeezes my shoulder and then leaves. Eventually a nurse comes in to speak with me, then the doctor. When they're not in the room, there's no sound except for Dad's machines. I know I should say something to him. The nurse and doctor both told me to speak to him, but hell, we don't know what to say to each other when everything is okay; him being in a coma doesn't make it easier.

Hours later my legs cramp from sitting so long and my pulse and breathing start going in rhythm with the sounds of the room. I'm humming them in my head, my legs getting twitchy now, and I realize if I don't leave this room, I'm going to go fucking insane.

"I'm sorry…for everything." They're the only words I've spoken to him, and then I'm out the door, rushing through the ICU and bursting through the doors and into the sterile, white hallway.

There's a heavy weight in my chest now, squashing my lungs so I can't breathe. One leg in front of the other, I move faster and faster until I'm running down the hallway. I'm thinking about how I couldn't speak to him, and that I didn't cry. Shouldn't I cry? Wouldn't most people cry?

Finally I burst through the doors. Drops of water splash onto my face as I stand in the gray, rainy Portland day. Everything feels heavy—the clouds, the sky, the air…me.

My clothes are soaked. My body's shivering, an earthquake under my skin. I can't fucking stop it, and I think maybe it'll help if I pretend the rain is my tears because at least then the reason I'm standing here alone would make sense. I wouldn't just be feeling all those useless years of silence echoing in my ears and wishing that I'd found words to share with him, when now it might be too late.

Then arms are around me from behind and I'm sagging into them. I know exactly who it is, but it's still a reassurance when I hear, "It's okay, I got you," in Levi's hushed voice.

Turning around, I ask, "What if he dies?" My hand knots in the back of his hoodie, the black one because he let me wear the one that says San Francisco State. I suddenly wish I had let him wear the one he wanted because he deserves that and more. I'm clutching him so tight my fingers hurt, and Levi's arms around me are squeezing with the same intensity.

We're both trembling as rain soaks our clothes, but I think I'd be okay standing with him here forever.

"He won't."

"You can't promise that."

"He won't." Levi grabs my face now, his hands cupping my cheeks. "Not like this. It's not fair. You won't lose him like this."

What in life is ever fair? It's not fair that my mom left or fair that my dad doesn't talk to me. It's not fair that Levi feels trapped. He's only twenty-fucking-four years old. He should have an open future and not be tied to anything. Fairness has nothing to do with our existence… But still, there's a part of me that wants to believe him. Not just because of my dad, but because it was Levi who said the words.

"Thank you," I tell him.

Through the rain I can still see Levi's eyes wrinkle around the edges. I love it when they do that. "For what?"

"For coming…for staying…I'm sure you would rather be home than sitting in a hospital waiting for me."

Levi's hands still hold my face. His thumb brushes my left cheek. His eyes darken and I hate that it's a familiar thing to see, hate that I'm the one who causes his disappointment and sadness. "You really think that, don't you?"

I shrug. "It's the hospital. Who wouldn't rather be at home instead of here?"

"I don't know what I'm going to do with you," he replies. "But Chris didn't understand why I would stay either. He made a big deal out of it. Apparently I'm not allowed to worry about you."

The storm beating down on us seems to find its way into my stomach. "You didn't tell him, did you?"

Levi drops his hands. "Are you kidding me right now? Of course I didn't. Your dad is in the hospital. You have a lot on your mind. I know this isn't the time to break the news that we're seeing each other, though I really don't think it should be a big deal. Chris can't care *that* much and we both know my parents won't. I have to admit though, I didn't like watching him pull you away without a glance at me like I don't fucking matter. I want to matter, Tobias, and I want people to know it."

"You matter."

"Do I?"

Words get trapped in my throat. My head starts spinning, fears reminding me this can't turn out well.

"Never mind. Now isn't the time. My balls are probably the size of grapes right now. It's cold and I'm wet and you need to focus on yourself and your dad. Come on, let's go inside and get changed."

Levi doesn't grab my hand, doesn't put an arm around me, just walks back toward the hospital. As the warmth of his touch quickly gets washed away by the rain, I realize how much better everything is when he's holding me.

CHAPTER THIRTY-FIVE

The next few days are tough. They do a scan on Dad and decide they want to give it a few more days and try some different medications before attempting to take him out of the coma. They're worried about his brain swelling and bleeding. Levi asks his dad a hundred questions about it. Tries to explain everything to me that's going on, and it just makes me even more in awe of him.

I've been staying at the hospital. Chris, Gemma, and Levi come every morning and spend most of the day with me. Every night, Levi tries to stay here with me, but I won't let him. He shouldn't have to spend his time sleeping on crappy waiting room chairs and eating shit food.

It's the fourth day, a Monday when all of us should be back at school. Gemma and Chris have gone to get some food. My mouth's dry as hell, and my eyes scratchy. I need something to wake me up or to curl up and go to sleep. My bones feel like they're filled with heavy metal, making me stiff and weighing me down.

"Do you want a coffee or something?" Levi asks.

Absolutely. "Yeah, thank you. That'd be great."

He gives me a small smile. "Okay. I'll be right back."

Levi's gone less than ten seconds when Elaine reaches over and lays a hand on mine. "It's you, isn't it?"

"Huh?" I look over at her, trying to figure out what she means.

"The boy Levi's in love with. It's you. I see it in the way he looks at you. The way he's trying to take care of you."

It's a stupid reaction but my head starts spinning. She knows. I can't believe she figured it out. What does this mean for us?

My dad could die, and all I can think about is that I can't handle losing someone else. Not my best friend because of my betrayal or Levi...because if it comes to me or his brother, who is he going to choose? "Um...we've been seeing each other, yeah. I'm sorry if that's a shock. We didn't really mean for it to happen."

When her eyes wrinkle around the edges I realize where Levi got the habit. "You sound like you think I would care. You know gay or straight doesn't matter to my family. And if I'm being honest, I'm thrilled that it's you. You've been like a part of our family for a very long time, Toby. We love you."

Those last three words somehow quiet the storm in my brain. I don't remember the last time I heard them. Not from Dad... Maybe from Mom before she left. It's all a blur now, I just know that I'm hearing them now from a woman who stepped up and was like a parent to me when mine struggled or disappeared.

"Thank you. I love you guys, too." Which is why this

229

scares me. I don't want to rock the boat and lose them. "Levi and I...we're not in love, though." Because if he was, he would have said it. Even if he thought he loved me, Levi would let those words out. He'd consider it weak not to. "It's just a...thing." Then I remember that she told Levi she hoped he wasn't being used for sex, so I scramble to say, "I mean, not that kind of thing. It's not like..." How in the hell do I tell someone's mom I'm not just using them for a piece of ass?

Elaine laughs a rich, happy laugh that also sounds like her son's. They're both such alive, happy, caring people. I didn't realize how similar they were until now.

"This could get into uncomfortable territory real quick. We should probably stop where we are and I'll just say I stick by my original assessment, okay? I'm happy and I know my son."

Smiling at her, I reply, "Okay." But she doesn't really know everything about Levi. She doesn't know he doesn't want to be a doctor. She doesn't know he takes medication for anxiety every day.

Levi shows up with my coffee a few minutes later. I mumble a "Thank you," but don't really look at him. It's strange now, knowing that his mom knows, wondering if she really does care at all, or if this will change things.

Chris and Gemma make their way back not long after Levi does. He's across the room from me, Chris on my right and Elaine on my left.

Levi says, "You should go home tonight, Tobias. You can't stay here every day. They'll call you with any updates." From across the waiting room, I lock eyes with him.

"He's right, sweetie." Elaine lays a hand on my thigh and

squeezes.

Chris nudges me from my other side. "I can stay at your place with you. Or you can come home with us. You just need to get out of here. It can't be good for you to stay."

They're right, I know it, but then the guilt sets in. I should be here. What if he wakes up? What if he dies? Hell, we screwed up everything in our lives enough. I don't want to fuck this up too.

"Toby," Levi says. "You deserve a break."

I don't know about that but I know I want one. Levi's words cement it. "Okay, I'll go home."

"Do you want me to stay with you?" Chris asks. Without looking, I know Levi's eyes are on me. It's a weak move, but I steer clear of glancing his way.

"Nah, thanks though. I think I need to be alone."

They drive me back to Coburn. The second I step into the lonely house, I know this is a mistake. It's so small, but I always feel lost here. Right now, I don't want to be lost. Don't want to be alone.

I sit in the same chair Dad sits in every day. I turn on a basketball game and pretend I give a shit about it. After it's over I make my way to the nearly empty fridge. The freezer is packed with frozen meals. The single magnet rattles and falls off when I slam the door. Then it's me going down, sliding to the floor and using the fridge to hold me up.

This is what he did. He sat in this house alone day after day without having a life, without getting close to anyone or making any kind of real connections. And now he could die, alone.

Fumbling with my phone, I call Levi. He hardly gets his "hello" out before I say, "I don't want to be alone tonight."

"I'm on my way."

I don't move from my spot on the kitchen floor, leaning on the fridge. A few minutes later, the knob on the front door shakes. As it pushes open, a deep breath escapes from my lungs.

"Tobias?" Levi calls.

"In the kitchen." His Nikes squeak on the floor. Without looking at him, I say, "I'm sorry."

"You don't need to be." He stops in front of me and holds out his hand. It makes me feel weak as hell, but I let him pull me to my feet. "You don't ever have to be alone. Why can't you see that? I'm here. Chris is here. Your dad loves you. My family loves you. You're not alone, baby, no matter how much you think you are. We're not going to leave."

And that's the crux of it all right there. Mom left. Dad doesn't know how to be there. It's a whole lot easier not to get close than it is to lose people you love.

"Come lay down with me." Levi threads his fingers through mine, leads me to my bedroom. He bends down and unties my shoes and then I kick out of them. He does the same to his. A minute later we're in my childhood bed in our underwear wrapped around each other. "I wish I could read your mind," Levi says as we cuddle in a cocoon of blankets. Fucking cuddle. I can't believe how much I've done that since getting with him.

"I wish you could, too." Because I care about him, I appreciate him. I'm in love with him, yet the words still trap themselves inside me.

"You don't get close to anyone. You let Chris in when you were a kid, but no one else. I know it's ridiculous for me to be jealous. You're friends, I know that, but it fucking eats away at me, rubs me raw that you picked him. That he's the one you let inside you and now you're so fucking scared to do it with anyone else. It's like you think there's a quota on your capacity for love and friendship. It's all surface stuff— fucking people you don't care about, not having real friendships with people like Xavier or Cherise."

"Lately—"

"Not letting me inside."

"You're here, Levi. I called you."

"I know." He growls into my neck. "I fucking love that I'm here with you. But I want to be that man for you out there, too. I want to walk you down the hall to see your dad. I want to bring you lunch to make you feel better. I want to tell everyone I'm taking you home to take care of you and not have to sneak out to do it. And I also know that throwing all of this on you right now makes me a dickhead. You have enough on your plate, but I can't keep going without being one hundred percent real about how I feel. I care a lot about you, more than you know. I can go my whole life living a lie in every aspect of it except that one."

"I..." have no fucking clue what to say to that. I care about him too. I'm in love with him. He's the only real flicker of joy inside me, this light that started out dim but grows by the second.

"Don't say anything right now. Like I said, you have shit on your mind, but know that when your dad heals, I'm not playing games anymore. You and I are going to get real about stuff soon. I won't hold it off anymore. I want more than your body. I want your heart and I need your words. I need to know you feel the same. I can't be in this alone."

CHAPTER THIRTY-SIX

The next couple days are spent at the hospital, but my nights are at home. Levi lies and tells Chris and his family he's going wherever it is he tells them he's going, but he comes to me. Every night. I keep expecting him not to be there, waiting for him to disappear or shut me out, but neither of those things has happened yet. Gemma had to go back to school. Every night Chris asks me to go to their house or if I want him to come to mine. I always say no and then I wait for his brother. I'm such a fucking liar.

It's Thursday morning and we're all sitting in the Baxter living room. Even Dr. Baxter is home this time. In a little while we'll go to Portland where Dad's going to have another test to see if they can start trying to bring him out of the coma.

Dr. Baxter leans against the couch with his arms crossed. He's not the kind of guy who tries to be intimidating, but he is. It's how he's built. "You need to head back to school, Levi. You've missed four days. It's nice of you to want to be here for your brother's friend, but this isn't an extended vacation here."

I freeze up and see Levi do the same from across the room.

"It's not going to hurt him to miss a few days," Elaine says waving her hand as if what Dr. Baxter said makes no sense.

"He's a second-year medical student at Stanford. Next year he starts his clinical rotations. Yes, dear, missing time can hurt him."

"You're not telling Chris to go back," Levi interrupts. "It's not a big deal, Dad. I'll be fine. I can make it up. If not this year, then I guess I'll find a way next year."

His father doesn't seem to agree. "No, you won't. You're going back. Like I said, it's nice of you to want to be here, but he has Chris." Levi flinches, and I can tell I'm not the only one who notices. Elaine closes her eyes, shakes her head. "His friend can support him," Dr. Baxter continues. "Medical school is different than Chris's program."

Aw, fuck. That's the worst thing he could say for both Chris and Levi. Can't he see how important Chris's life is, too? See that Levi doesn't have to follow the same exact path his father followed?

"So what Levi's doing is more important than what I'm doing?" Chris jumps in. "Stupid question. Of course it is. Everything Levi does is always more important because Levi's perfect. Everyone wants to be like him, and everyone loves him. I'm just Chris. I don't matter."

"Now everyone calm down. This is the last thing Toby needs," Elaine says, but Dr. Baxter's voice rises over hers.

"Don't do that, Christopher. Don't put words into my mouth. Your schooling is very important, but we can all admit that it's not the same as medical school."

"Of course not!" Chris tosses his arms up and then lets them drop heavily against his sides. "I'm so tired of the whole damn world revolving around Levi!"

That's enough to make Levi turn to him. "What the hell are you talking about? The world doesn't revolve around me. You don't know the shit I deal with."

"Are you kidding me right now? What the hell do you have to deal with?"

My stomach sinks deeper and deeper every second. This is the last thing I want, causing drama in their family, making people fight. "It's fine," I say. "Everyone can go back to school. I'm good. No one needs to screw up their grades for me. It'll probably be easier if I'm by myself anyway. I don't want to be a burden."

Levi whips my direction, fire igniting in his eyes. "Don't do that, Tobias. Don't play the 'I'm an island, I don't need anyone' bullshit right now." He's pleading with me. Every part of him is. I see it in the desperation in his eyes, the way he looks at me and leans toward me. The way his body almost slumps over. He needs me to be honest, needs me to show him I want him. And I do, so fucking much it's become a constant ache inside me that only Levi has the cure for, but my dad is in the hospital and Chris is seething with anger. It's all too much. I can't deal with this right now. I can't make Chris understand.

"No offense, Dad, but you can't make me go. I'm an adult." And then to me and only me, he adds, "I'm not leaving, no matter what."

Thank you.

237

NYRAE DAWN

"Why? Because the great and powerful Levi can make it better?" Sarcasm plays off every one of Chris's words.

Just as my stomach rolls, Levi snaps back, "No, asshole, because I'm in love with him. What the hell is your problem with me, anyway? What did I ever do to you that's so bad? Is this because of Bridget?"

In love with me... In some ways he basically said the same thing when we were in my bed. He was warning me. I get that, but hearing him say the words, with his whole family around is a different thing.

Damned if I don't want it to be true. Maybe even need it. "Levi...I..." When I don't continue, he shakes his head.

"Are you serious? You're with my brother?" Chris says pulling my attention from Levi. His eyes shoot daggers at me. I can read him the same way I did Levi and he's ready to explode. His jaw's tight, a vein pulsing in his temple.

"You're gay?" Dr. Baxter asks Levi. There's no anger in his voice just...surprise, and maybe a little bit of frustration because Dr. Baxter doesn't like surprises. He likes everything to run through him.

"I don't see the problem here," Elaine adds. "It's Toby and Levi."

No one speaks, everyone waiting on me. Or at least Levi and Chris are. There are so many things I can say right now. So many things I need to say but they all get clogged up in my throat. "I'm sorry, Chris," is all I can find.

"You're sorry for being with me?" Levi asks.

I turn from Chris to face him. "What? No. I'm sorry for lying to him."

"How long have you been lying to me?" When my eyes find Chris again, I can see him putting it all together. "He was at your house the past few nights, wasn't he?"

"Yeah," I say. There's a sadness to my voice that feels like a betrayal of Levi. But I can't help it. I feel as though I've betrayed Chris, too, and there's no way I can hold back on my misery for failing either one of them.

"And let me guess, he's the reason you bailed on spring break and the concert... Holy shit, he gave you a gift at Christmas. You've been lying that fucking long?"

"Don't speak like that in my house, Chris. I don't care how old you are." No one looks at Dr. Baxter. No one gives him a reply. That has to be a first.

"He hated doing it, man. We didn't mean for all this to happen," Levi says to his brother.

"Don't. Don't tell me who my best friend is. I know him." His angry gaze bounces from his brother to me. "Or at least I used to. Jesus, Toby. We've spent eleven fucking years being best friends. I've always had your back and you've been lying to me for Levi?"

I still can't find my words.

"Why do you hate me so much?" Levi's facing Chris and I can hear the pain as his voice breaks on the question. My heart breaks, too. Everything inside me wants to go to him, to touch him and comfort him the way he's done to me, but I don't move. Chris is hurting. Levi is. I am. This whole thing has turned into a giant clusterfuck.

"Your brother doesn't hate you," his mom tells him, but Chris isn't having it.

Glaring at Levi, he opens his mouth and I know a lifetime of history is about to be laid out. "Because you get fucking everything! You're smarter, and everyone loves you. You're the better son because you want to be a doctor, which means nothing I ever do will be as good as what you're doing!" Chris yells. "There wasn't one person in my life who ever cared about me more than you before Toby. You took girls I wanted and friends I wanted, and now you stole my best friend as well." Chris turns to me. "And fuck you for letting him. You should have told me, Toby. I would have gotten over it if you didn't lie."

"I didn't choose him over you." And I didn't. Chris will always be my boy.

"Christopher, you have to know that isn't true," Elaine says, but Chris doesn't reply to either of us. He just walks out.

"I'm sorry, Levi, Toby," Elaine says, her voice shaky. "I need to check on him." She goes out right behind him.

When I turn around, Levi's sitting on the beige couch, elbows on his knees and face in his hands.

"I apologize," Dr. Baxter tells him. "I didn't understand the nature of your relationship with Toby. You have feelings for him, and I understand you wanting to support him, Levi. That's an honorable thing to do, but that doesn't change the fact that you need to be in school. I'm sure Toby understands and wants what's best for you, don't you?" He looks at me, and there's only one answer he expects to hear. He's a good man and has always treated me well, but he's also used to having the last say. He's used to being obeyed.

Dr. Baxter wants his answer, but as I look over at Levi, I know he wants another. He wants me to tell him to stay… But

I have to wonder—why can't he tell his dad why he really doesn't want to go? Why does it just have to be about me? This is his chance to tell his dad how he feels about being a doctor.

Still, he sits there watching me, pleading with me. The same feelings are probably mirrored in my eyes.

"No response. I don't know why I'm surprised." Levi stands. "I just found out my brother sincerely hates me, and the man I love probably won't ever be able to be honest about the way he feels about me, but thanks for being worried about that, Dad. I'll be sure to get right back down to school because we all know that's the only thing that's important."

And then Levi walks away from me too. I've never felt more like my dad. Alone. Left behind.

CHAPTER
THIRTY-SEVEN

For the next couple days, I don't leave the hospital. My mind's a massive tangle of too many thoughts to sort through—Levi, Chris, Dad. Every time I try to figure things out, try to unravel everything that's happened, it's like my circuits overload and my emotions and my body shut down. It's all I can do to find the strength to get up and try again.

It's one of those days where I'm struggling for strength, when I hear a soft knock on my dad's hospital room door.

It's ajar already, but there's a sweet voice that says, "Knock knock. Can I come in?"

Taking a deep breath I turn to look at Elaine, forcing myself to smile. "Hi, yeah. Come in." Standing up, I point to the chair so she can sit down, but she just shakes her head.

"No, thank you."

I don't sit down again, and I'm shifting nervously from foot to foot, when she says, "My husband tells me they're bringing him out of the coma. That's good news."

"Yeah." Shoving my hands into my pockets, I wait for

her to say what she came to say.

She looks up at me through eyes the same dark-whiskey color as Levi's. "I'm sorry about everything that happened the other day, kiddo."

"Thank you." I am too. "Did they head out? Did Levi go back to school?" The room goes still while I wait for her response. I swear even the fucking machines seem to quiet, waiting to hear about Levi. Typical.

"Yes." She fidgets with her purse. "They both left. Levi that day and Chris yesterday."

There's a pang in my chest. It starts out as a little nick, a pebble hitting a windshield, but it grows out from there. Each second it spiders out, another long crack running the length of me. Of course he went back. Why shouldn't he? Oh, other than the fact that regardless of what happened with us, medical school is the last place Levi wants to be.

"They'll come around, both of them. They love you. You should call them," Mrs. Baxter says.

But I can't, not right now. I spent the last six months lying to my best friend, and as for Levi...I saw it in his eyes when he walked away. He finally realized I can't give him what he needs. "You should talk to Levi," I tell her. "Really talk to him. He deserves to be happy."

She nods slowly, goodbye in her eyes. "I will. Thanks, Toby. If you need anything, let me know. Anything at all, okay?"

I close my eyes when she hugs me, hold her a second longer than she does me, and then back away. "Thanks, Mrs. B."

And then just like everyone else, she's gone.

CHAPTER
THIRTY-EIGHT

It's the middle of the night when Dad wakes up. His eyes flutter, try to adjust, before they land on me. My heart lurches, crawls up my throat as I shove to my feet, and lean over the bed.

"Hey, Dad. Hi. It's Toby." No shit it's fucking Toby. Who the hell else would it be?

He opens his mouth, but nothing comes out, and then there's a nurse there pushing me out of the way and checking him out.

It goes like that for a few days. He's awake more and more but can't really talk. His throat's sore from where he was intubated and a few other reasons they tell me but I don't pay attention to most of them. All I know is he can't talk, and not in the same way we didn't speak before.

With each minute that passes, each hour, each day, Dad's getting more and more frustrated.

It takes another couple days for him to get his voice back. Still it's soft, rough from lack of use, when he says, "Wallet. In. My. Wallet."

There's a cabinet with his things in it on the other side of the room. I kept meaning to take most of it home, but kept forgetting. I don't want to get up though, don't want to walk away from him because he's alive and looking at me and talking. I want us to grab onto our words now, say everything that needs to be said because I could have fucking lost him and I wouldn't have had the chance to tell him I loved him. *I would always wonder if he loved me...*

"Please," Dad says, so I force myself to my feet and hurry to the cabinet. It sticks, so I pull harder and it makes a slight popping sound before coming open. I glance over at Dad who's watching me...who's smiling at me.

My fingers fumble to open the bag where they've stashed his things. Finally I get it open, and then pull his wallet out before going back to sit beside his bed again.

"Open." He points to it, nodding at me, a smile still on his thick lips, which are shaped like mine.

There's an old envelope inside. It's bent from being folded in his wallet so long, the corners tearing and the page weathered where it's creased. My name is scrawled on it in the same messy handwriting that was on my Christmas card. This has been there much longer, though.

Looking up at him, my brows pull together. I'm wondering what's in this letter that he's held onto for so long.

"Read." He nods toward my hand.

With shaky fingers I rip it open.

Tobias,

I have a confession to make, that I probably should have made a long time ago. It's hard for me...words don't come real easily to me, which I'm sure comes as no surprise to you. It's always been a problem for me made even worse by my guilt.

The truth is, I asked your mama to leave.

My eyes jerk from the paper and land squarely on my dad. What the fuck? He asked her to go? He told her to leave us...to leave me? "Why?" My voice snaps like a feral dog on the attack.

"Read," he says again and as much as I want to force him to tell me, to fucking speak instead of taking the easy way out, I know he can't right now. So I fight to steady my hand, to hold the aged paper still so I can continue to read.

Sometimes I wonder how much you remember. You've never said much and Lord knows I haven't opened up to you. Do you remember that the last time she left wasn't the first? That she had stints where she'd be gone for weeks at a time and Grandma would come stay with us, or I'd have to take time off work? Do you remember that sometimes she would sleep for days on end?

She went into rehab four times over the years, each one because I insisted. The first time I'd come home from work to see she'd left food cooking and you in front of the television. She'd be passed out in the bathroom. You were five. I'm thankful if you don't remember.

The words begin to blur, to swim around the page, forcing me to wipe my eyes so I can see them clearly. Tiny shards of memories start coming together in my head...the time I couldn't wake her, the time we snuck out of bed while Dad was sleeping and we ate a whole loaf of bread, making sandwich after sandwich until I got sick.

There's more, if you want we'll talk about it. The last day I had a double shift at work. She knew I wouldn't be home until after three a.m. You waited for her to pick you up at school, and she didn't come. You walked home and sat in that house all day and half the night scared while she was out struggling with her demons.

That, I knew—I knew she'd forgotten about me and left me alone. That she picked a day Dad wouldn't be home to disappear, but I hadn't let myself call him.

When I walked into that house and saw you curled up on the couch, crying, something broke inside me, Tobias. I loved her so much, I wanted to save her so badly... but I loved you more. You were more important. So I put you to bed, and when she came home, I told her she had to go back into rehab, or she couldn't come back.

I've spent the last eleven years wondering if I made the right decision. If I robbed you of your mother. If I robbed you of your family because Lord knows I haven't been the kind of father you deserve.

I'm a flawed man, kid. I will never claim to be anything different, but I love you, and I'm sorry I'm not better at showing you that.

I squeeze my eyes shut, trying to make sense of it all. Trying to hold back the tears. She had a problem. She could have hurt me. Dad asked her to leave. He did it because he loves me. She chose her addiction over us.

"Toby. I love you."

With those four words spoken aloud, every hard edge in me softens, every stitch in my armor dissolves until there's nothing else, just raw, open Tobias Jackson, and I cry. My eyes pool, blur, then brim over as I grab my dad's hand and say, "I love you, too."

He squeezes my hand and I squeeze his. Tears run down his face, wetting his pillow as we hold each other and cry. Things aren't perfect. I'm not sure what I feel, and there's a million questions I need to ask. There's talking to do, and healing to be done, but now that the gate's been opened, our words set free, I won't ever let either of us close them again.

We're on the right path, Dad and I, now I just need to find the right path for myself as well.

CHAPTER THIRTY-NINE

I open the door to my apartment to see Xavier sitting on the couch, phone in his hand. "There's someone in our apartment complex on Grindr right now. Have you seen anyone blow-worthy around here? His abs look nice from the picture."

I smile, relief flooding through me. It's good to be home. "I missed you, too."

Xavier tosses his cell to the coffee table. "How's your pops?"

"On the mend."

"You said you missed me. We really are friends now, huh?" He winks, his eyes looking different when there's no dark eyeliner on them. He's trying to be nonchalant, and I appreciate that but there's too much heavy shit inside me to be nonchalant, too. I need to let it out, don't want it trapped inside me to fester anymore. Dad let too many things rot his will to be happy for too long; I can't let that become me.

"We are... I'm going to try not to be such a dickhead most of the time."

"Why? Dicks are fun."

Rolling my eyes at him, I sit down on our small couch. Dropping my head back, I say, "Everything's so fucked up, man. I screwed things up with Levi and my best friend isn't talking to me. My dad's in the hospital and I found out some shit about my past that I'm still trying to sort through." But I can't do it alone...and I need to dig through it. Turning my head, I look at him. "I could use a friend."

Xavier shrugs. "I'm sittin' right here."

And I know it's not just him who's there for me—Cherise and Brian would be there, too. I have people in my corner; I just have to make sure not to push them away.

Sitting on our faded, dirty couch with a video game in the background and stale smoke clinging to the air, I talk to Xavier. I tell him how I screwed up with Levi and pushed him away. Tell him about my lies and my shit growing up. He sits there and listens, waits, lets me lean on him and when I finish he says, "Your boy loves you. Get your shit together up here." Xavier taps his temple with a finger, "And right here," then his chest. "Then you make things right with everyone else. Shit's gotta be right with you first."

And I know he's right.

CHAPTER FORTY

June

The phone doesn't stop ringing.

Chris used to be quick to answer, but as the number of rings climbs—three, four—fear claws at me. He's not going to answer. I waited too fucking long. I lost my best friend.

"Hello?"

And then I can breathe. "Hey…it's me."

"No shit. Did you think I lost your number? Deleted it from my phone? I've been waiting for your punk ass to call. Took you long enough."

Jesus, I missed the sound of his fucking voice. "I screwed up."

"I know."

"I didn't mean to hurt you."

"I know that, too."

"You're my best friend."

"No shit."

Then I'm laughing and Chris is doing the same. When we finally calm down, he says, "I was angry…probably more than I should have been. It's just, you know how shit with me and Levi was. I was jealous and being a pussy like always when it comes to him. Still, you should have told me. I wouldn't lie to you, never have. That's not cool, T."

This time it's me who's saying, "I know." My bed squeaks when I sit down. My room's full of boxes that Cherise and Brian helped me pack. "I'm sorry. I know it sounds crazy, but I was scared to lose you if you found out. I wanted him, but I knew I needed you, too."

"Do you really think I'd walk away from eleven years of friendship because you have shitty taste in dudes?"

As much as I don't want to fight with Chris, not anymore, I can't keep quiet about Levi either. "He's a good guy. He's not who you think he is. He's…"

"I know. We're working on our stuff. I see that it wasn't all him, he was going through more than I thought and maybe some things had been misinterpreted. That doesn't mean we're perfect, but we're better. A lot of shit's gone down since I've been waiting for you to make the first move. I'll admit, I understand why you were nervous to tell me, but I don't get how you could really think you'd lose me. I'm not going anywhere, T."

He's not. Logically, I know that. Our bond is too strong. "I get it. I just couldn't believe it. I'm working on that, though. Been talking to someone, trying to learn that everyone I love isn't going to leave."

There's a long pause and then, "Are you in love with

Levi?"

My eyes don't veer away from his easel in the corner,
Levi's easel. "Yeah." There's nothing I've been surer of in
my life.

"Then you should tell him." Chris chuckles. "I can't
believe my brother was fucking you. This is going to take
some getting used to." It's the best thing he can say, the
realest.

"How do you know I wasn't fucking him?"

"Ah, shit. Too much information." He makes a gagging
noise through the phone. He and Levi both have this youthful,
fun quality about them. They're more alike than they realize.
Or hell, maybe they do realize it now.

"Are you going home this summer?" I ask.

"Yeah, in a couple weeks. I'm going to spend some time
with Gem's family first."

"Can we meet up when you get home? I won't be there
all summer, but some of it."

"No shit. You owe me more of an explanation, and to
hang out because you ditched me to screw my brother,
apparently." There's a rustling sound on the other end of the
phone and then Chris adds, "On the real though, of course.
You're my boy. I love you."

"I love you too, man." Some of the weight in my chest
dissolves. One down, one to go.

"Now go sweep my brother off his feet or whatever the
fuck it is you guys do."

"He could have moved on."

"You'll never know till you try, will you?" And then Chris hangs up.

This sudden urgent, wild need claws at me. My muscles spasm, little jolts of electricity shooting through them, propelling me from the bed, through the apartment and out the door.

I don't stop until I get to the Baby Bullet train station.

Address??? I text Chris.

Jesus, I don't even know where Levi lives. I was a shitty boyfriend. He deserves so much better than the way I treated him.

Chris sends the information back almost immediately. The thirty-seven minutes it takes the train to get to Palo Alto drags. I've waited weeks and now I'm going to burst at the fucking seams if I don't talk to Levi right now.

Once off the train, it takes another five minutes for an Uber car to pick me up. I give them Levi's address and it feels like one of those lame-ass movies where some dude is paying a cab to hurry and get him to his lover before they jump on a plane to leave forever.

Only I don't know if Levi's going anywhere. I don't even know if he still wants me, but I sure as fuck still want him.

His apartment complex is a million times nicer than the one Xavier and I live in. My heart's in my throat as I make my way to his door, no damn clue what I'm going to say when I get there.

And then I'm knocking and I hear his scratchy voice call out, "Just a sec!"

I'm fidgeting and breathing heavy and being way too over dramatic, but at this point, I don't care.

He pulls open the door, his eyes landing squarely on me. He has a T-shirt on that's tight across his chest, and his brown hair is hanging down on his forehead like always. He's fucking beautiful.

"Hey." Hey? All I can say is hey?

"Hey."

"Can I come in?"

Levi shrugs. "Sure." Then he turns around, leaving the door open. I follow him, closing it behind us, and watch as he sits on the couch.

"Nice place." The walls are crisp and clean, the carpet nice. The furniture looks new, but there's also boxes scattered around the room. On the shelf to the far right sits one thing— the owl he bought when we went to the pier. "Going somewhere?"

"Maybe."

"Home for the summer?"

"Nope. Moving. I can't afford this place anymore." Oh shit. That can't be good.

"I'm sorry." I take a step toward him but Levi's eyes narrow, reminding me I lost the right to touch him, to comfort him.

"What are you doing here, Toby?" He stretches out his long legs casually, making panic shoot through me. Making guilt eat at me as well. How many times did I ask him the same kind of question? It doesn't feel good being on the other end of it.

"I'm here to tell you I'm sorry." I take a step closer, can't seem to force myself to keep away. "I'm here because I missed you. I missed you since the day I forced you to walk away from me."

"Then why did you do it? Why the hell couldn't you just admit you fucking want me?" His voice rides the air, vibrating through me, leaving shame in its wake.

"Because I screwed up. Because I was scared. I know those are shitty excuses, but they're true."

"And I wasn't scared?" Levi's body jerks forward so he's sitting up straight. "I was out-of-my-fucking-mind afraid, but I was there. I had a million other things in my head, but I was still fucking in it, Tobias. One hundred and ten percent. I was patient and I waited and tried not to push you. I can't wait anymore. Can't wait to live my life."

He's right. He's so fucking right. No one should have to wait for someone else to be happy. He shouldn't be in school for something he's unsure about, and he definitely doesn't need to wait for me.

And I can't put off saying things that need to be said, either. "She was supposed to pick me up from school the day she left. She never showed. I walked home, stayed there, scared all night. She made me a fucking sandwich that morning like it was any other day and then I just never saw her again."

He closes his eyes, pain obvious in his tense features, but I don't stop there. Can't. I tell him everything. I tell him about crying on the couch that night. My dad losing himself more and more. Feeing alone, the fear of being left. I tell him about the letter Dad wrote and the conversations we've had since. Shoving my hands into my pockets and watching him, I tell him about her stints in rehab they tried to hide from me. How I maybe blocked some shit out.

Levi's quiet, listening, his features getting softer by the second. He's so fucking beautiful and I wish with all my heart that I could crawl inside him and live there.

Finally after spilling my guts so long my throat's dry and my legs hurt from standing up, I say, "I'm not the only one though, Levi. Most of the problems with us are my fault, but you have things to work out, too."

For the first time since I walked into his place, a smile cracks on his face. "Do I now?"

I risk another step closer to him, then another. He's still sitting down, legs out as he leans against the back of the couch.

"You gotta be happy," I tell him. "We both have to be happy in our lives if we're going to be happy together...not that you said you want to be together, but I do, so I'm pushing for that." I wink at him. "I like to get my way the same as you." He gives me another small smile, but I can see he's trying to hide it. I keep talking. "You didn't give up on me before and I'm not giving up on you now. I fucked up. I treated you like shit. You deserved better, but I'm telling you right now it wasn't because I don't want you. I'm crazy in love with you, Levi, and that scares the shit out of me. I thought if I didn't put myself out there, I couldn't get hurt, but even if I do—" I shrug. "—you're worth it."

This time, he doesn't try to hide the grin that stretches across his face. "That was a good speech."

"Yeah?" I ask. "I have more. Dad and I have been talking, really fucking talking. I talked to the counselor at the school as well. I'm still a work in progress, but I want to put in that work with you, Levi. I was afraid to give you my words before, but I'm not scared anymore. I'll give you a hundred thousand words every day if that's what it takes to get you back. I love you."

"Get your ass over here, Tobias." The rest of the tension in my chest is gone, leaving nothing left but him. I do as he says and finish closing the space between us. I straddle his lap and he wraps his arms around me. All my life I wanted something to love. I thought I would find it someplace or somewhere, but not in another person because people can leave. But I thought wrong. I found love in Levi.

"You hurt me," he says. "Jesus, you hurt me."

Closing my eyes, I pull him tight against me. He buries his face in my neck. "I know. I'm sorry. I'm so fucking sorry. I never wanted to hurt you. I love you. I'll make it up to you."

"Just be here. That's all you gotta do. I love you, too…and thank you."

Pushing his hair out of his face, I kiss his temple. "Digging the I love you, and even the thank you, but not sure what you have to thank me for."

"For time, I guess. I needed it, too. For coming back, for making me see that it's okay to fail…to screw up."

"Because I did that so spectacularly?" I ask.

"Maybe. I just… You made me happy. I wanted to hold onto that. I was fucked when I felt like you chose Chris over me, that you'd never really choose me. I came back here and I kept thinking of you and that stupid fucking play. How Jack and Algernon made up these fake personas, and that's what I was doing. I was tired of living that way. I talked to Chris, then my parents. They know it all—the anxiety, my fear, the fact that I'm not sure who in the fuck I am."

"Maybe you're not just one thing. Do we really have to be just one thing? Do you really have to know right now?" We're fucking young. We have our whole lives ahead of us. Why do society and our parents make us think we have to have all the answers right now?

"Shh." He presses his finger to my lips. "I'm getting there. I realized the same thing. I'm taking a year off of med school. I'm enrolled in art school for next year, which I have to pay for myself. From there I'll decide what I want. Maybe I'll be a doctor, maybe I'll do something that has to do with art. Maybe I won't do either of those things. I just know how it felt to walk away from you and I don't want to walk away from anything I care about again. The only way to find exactly what I want in my life is to try different things."

"Your dad?" I ask him.

"We're not on speaking terms right now. He's pissed. Hence the moving out. He won't pay for this apartment anymore. He's not going to be helping me as much, which is okay. I'm grown. I should be doing this shit on my own anyway."

"Fuck...that sucks. He helps Chris."

"That's because Chris didn't go to school for one thing for five years only to possibly change his mind." Levi shrugs. "I'll figure it out. But right now I really wanna taste you."

"Took you long enough." I cover Levi's mouth with mine, the familiar taste of him on my tongue again. He grabs my ass and we just sit there kissing. We stop every few minutes to talk. He's still going to school in San Francisco next year, which makes me really fucking happy.

I kiss him again, and we talk some more—important shit, not important shit. It doesn't matter. I just want to talk to him, to be close to him...hopefully fuck him again, but first, it's just our mouths in action...kissing and words.

He's taking a road trip home for the summer and asks me to ride with him. He tells me he's sorry for leaving me, that he'll never leave again, but I tell him he didn't have a choice. He didn't really walk away because I hadn't really given myself to him.

He kisses me again.

We talk more about his dad and mine. How Dad's leaving at the end of the summer to live with his mom in Tennessee. Levi says I should go with him for a week or so, and I think he's right.

What kind of life is it if you don't let yourself experience it? If you don't go for what you want and live how you want? If you don't open your mouth and say what's important and cling to those you love? Not being who you are, or saying how you feel, or fighting for what you love, not being willing to risk your heart, is losing by default.

I won't ever lose that way, and I know the man writhing under me with all his fucking passion for life won't either.

EPILOGUE

"We didn't plan this very well," is the first thing I say to Levi when I open the apartment door. "The couch looks good right there," comes afterward, as I take in what he's done with the living room.

Maybe it's stupid to get a place together this soon. Maybe we'll fight like crazy. Maybe we're rushing it.

Maybe we don't care, because maybe it'll be the best fucking thing in the world to live with each other and see each other every day between school and work and life.

See? Living the way we want. That's what we're doing.

"Glad you like it. We didn't have many options on the couch. The room is small. And who cares if we planned the timing well? Kiss me, baby. I haven't seen you in two weeks."

The second the door is closed, Levi has me backed against it. Our tongues are tangling. I have a hand in his hair and his is on my hip, and it's so damn awesome to have a boyfriend I want to be around all the time.

Knock, knock, knock.

"Fuck. I told you we didn't plan this very well."

Levi shrugs and adjusts his erection. "It is what it is. I missed you."

"I missed you, too."

Things have been a bit rushed. I went to Oregon to see my dad and then drove across the country with him. He's settled with Grandma now, and trying to find some kind of life. We're hoping the change of scenery helps. That and the fact that he's finally admitted something is wrong and is seeing a doctor. He's depressed. He knows it and I know it, it just took him a long time to get on the path to good mental health. He's there now and I couldn't be more proud of him.

While I was gone, Levi moved us into our new dump not far from my old one with the help of Xavier, Cherise and Brian. We spent the rest of the summer staying in my old place with Xavier.

Knock, knock.

"Going to answer that?" Levi cocks a brow at me.

"Sorry. Distracted." Turning around I pull open the door for Gemma and Chris.

"What up?" Chris asks and hugs me, then walks in and gives his brother a hug as well. Gemma does the same.

The four of us hang out and chat before going out to find something to eat. They crash at our house for the weekend, Levi and I playing hosts, while we explore the city, riding the trolley with them and all that shit. Gemma's never been to San Francisco before and it looks as though she's fallen in love with the place like we did.

Chris and Gemma leave Monday morning, heading back East for school and I'm naked, sweaty in bed with Levi fucking Baxter.

My Levi. It feels pretty damn good to think.

"I can't believe I'm not going to med school next week," he says after a period of silence.

"Are you scared?"

"Yeah."

Threading my fingers through his hair, I let out what's on my mind. "I think maybe the best things are scary. They test us, they're not easy, but that's the only way to tell if they're worth it."

"Oooh. My boyfriend is so fucking smart." Levi kisses my chest, the tattoo on my arm, and then down to my stomach.

"Shut up."

"No."

"Yes."

"No."

"Will you ever stop arguing with me?"

He's still kissing me as he chuckles. "Nope. Love givin' you shit. Love making up with you, too. You're right, though. The things that matter aren't easy. Not most of the time."

But just like facing my past and opening myself up to a future with him, they're worth it.

"Can I take you now?" He asks. "I think I've recovered."

"Yes."

"Good. We can have sex, then I'll draw you and then I'll feed you. We have to take advantage of days in bed before we're back to the grind."

It sounds like the perfect life to me.

THE END

ACKNOWLEDGEMENT

I feel so lucky to have some of the best friends in my corner. Kelley York and Wendy Higgins…what would I do without you? You talk me off more ledges than you know. Thanks for always being there for me.

Thanks to Matt Dellisola for letting me send you little snippets when I needed to and for being willing to talk things out with me. Glad to say I can call you a friend.

Huge thanks goes to Lenore Kosinski, Kim Marshall, Judy Zweifel, Sarah Arthur, Heather Young-Nichols, Christina Lee, Jessica de Ruiter, and Hope Cousin for your extra sets of eyes and for helping me to make Toby and Levi's story shine. I appreciate you so much.

Jamie Manning, thank you for always being there when I need to talk. You're one of the best guys I know.

Edie Danford, your edits were beautiful. I owe you all the thanks in the world.

Last…to my readers. It's been a long journey filled with too many ups and downs and twists and turns for me to count. You kept me going. Your support means more to me than I can ever say.

ABOUT THE AUTHOR

When not playing with her kids or spending time with her husband, Nyrae Dawn can almost always be found with a book in her hand or an open document on her laptop.

She gravitates toward character-driven stories. She's a proud romantic who has a soft spot for flawed characters who aren't perfect and make mistakes. Her motto is *be kind* and she believes in following your heart.

Nyrae is living her very own happily-ever-after in California with her gorgeous husband and two incredible kids.

She's written for Grand Central Publishing, Entangled Publishing, Harmony Ink, and is self-published. She's represented by Jane Dystel. You can find her online at http://www.nyraedawn.net

OTHER BOOKS BY NYRAE DAWN

NEW ADULT:

RUSH

CHARADE

FAÇADE

MASQUERADE

YOUNG ADULT:

THE HISTORY OF US

OUT OF PLAY

SEARCHING FOR BEAUTIFUL

And more…

A HUNDRED THOUSAND WORDS

Made in the USA
Columbia, SC
06 June 2020

10318868R00148